Pilgrims with Blades

A01 – Pressed into Service

(A novel set in the realm of Dhea Loral)

Douglas Van Dyke Jr.

Pilgrims with Blades
A01 - Pressed into Service

This edition published through Ingram

ISBN: 9781949060010
BISAC FIC009020 Fiction: Fantasy – Epic

PUBLISHED BY Douglas Van Dyke Jr
Please Visit:
http://dhealoral.com

Retail Price: $12.00

Preview

The others turned their attention back to the distant fighting. Vanford's prediction about the lack of an organized defense by the orcs appeared to be accurate. Kashmer forces swarmed up the beach and into cover with few casualties. There may have been only orc scouts on the shore, though it felt as if eyes were behind every rock. The boats returned, allowing group eighteen their chance to join the landing forces. Allisee and Vallese descended the rope ladder gracefully.

As Cruso put hands on the ladder, Mornik spoke. "After the time and effort I spent helping you buckle on all that metal, you better not slip and fall into that water."

"I am touched by your concern, good priest, but fear not. I am less burdened than I might appear." Sir Cruso replied as he swung his legs over the edge.

He wore the full suit of armor. Shield strapped to his back along with the silver sword, steel sword at his side, folded crossbow on his opposite hip; half the group feared they would be watching him drop and drown. The knight climbed down with ease, showing no impairment from his metal shell. Cruso took hold of one of the spare oars.

Mornik proved to have more trouble. The dwarf priest cursed in his native tongue as the rope ladder shook. Similar to the knight, Mornik had numerous items strapped to his body, but he failed to carry his weight as well as Cruso

"Watch yer own descent, Heavyboot!" Urgosk called from above. "Ha-ra, ha-ra!"

Both Allisee and Vallese gripped the sides of the boat with concern. Cruso and one of the rowers helped Mornik down the last couple steps. In comparison, Urgosk practically ran down the climbing ladder with ease. Only at the last rung did he falter and cry out, "Ah, help!" The boat rocked as everyone reacted at once, moving toward or away from him. But his exclamation proved a ruse, and he lithely dropped to a seat and grabbed an oar. He openly chuckled as the rest resumed their seats and the boat settled.

Vallese admonished, "This not play time!"

Urgosk, between chuckles, replied. "We live, we endure hard times and fear, then we die. Somewhere in that existence ya have to make time to laugh, or what good is life?"

Mornik, glaring at Urgosk, commented. "Hard to believe someone can be so wise yet so stupid at the same time."

Acknowledgments

My appreciation to Obsidian Abnormal for his work on the cover art. He went so far as to create individual posters of each protagonist before combining them for the cover. I'd also like to thank Denise Guibord for all her editing and suggestions. I have a better story thanks to her! Of course, I can't overlook the fans who have given me such great reviews on my previous work, as well as given me likes and shares on social media. You are my best advertising!

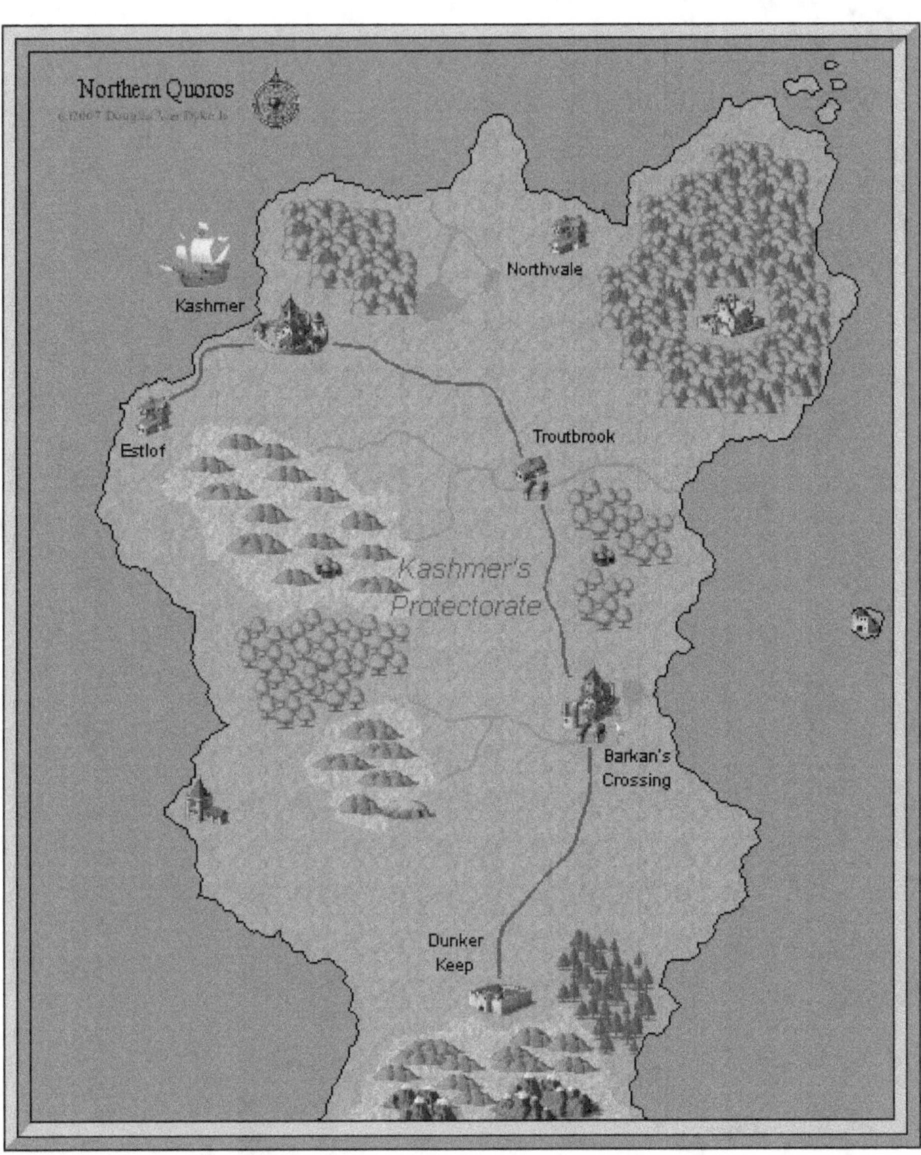

Northern Quoros
Kashmer
Estlof
Northvale
Troutbrook
Kashmer's Protectorate
Barkan's Crossing
Dunker Keep

For my long-running home campaign group. We've shared treasure and character deaths together. We enjoyed many laughs, developed many interesting characters and plotlines, and made memories to last a lifetime. I'd find it hard to write about an adventurous group of rascals and their misadventures without drawing inspiration from you.

Brian, Jennifer, Carrie and Bryce VanDyke
Phil, Myles, Gavin and Hudson Matz
Jeremy and Angie King
Kirk and Tony Coughlin
…and many more that go back nearly thirty years!

In his dream, the dwarf was actually a giant. His strides covered miles at a time, stretching across fiefdoms and cities with each step. His boots could cross deep ocean waters without passing his knee. The realm of Dhea Loral lie before him like a miniature model. A quick step from home and he overlooked Orlaun, the City of Spires. Full of cultures and a mix of races, it bustled with the markets of trade. Yet, for all its riches it didn't offer the welcome he would need.

Turning to the east, he slogged through the sea channels to a new land. He looked upon the entirety of the unexplored Wilderean Continent. The ancient trees scratched and tore through his leggings. He would not find what he needed here. He felt the familiar twinge of desperation.

Thus he marched across more seas, continents and countries. The Counties of Diara. The Republic of Lar. The Commonwealth of Jhuto. Each one offered naught. What he needed was missing. His need drove him to search farther.

The continent of Shri-Keya offered hope. There was a glimpse of mountains and warm hearths within. From mountains to shorelines, the tiny people he saw fought savagely with one another. One side consisted of those of his race. He thought he would find a welcome, but they rebuked anyone who was not of their clans. "No outsiders," they growled.

The journey had already taken too long. His legs could barely carry him. Wearily, he trudged back to the halls of his clan. Failure weighed on him. His kin would console and support him for his search, but his failure to find a solution doomed them all. His steps shortened, and in the dream his form steadily shrank toward a normal height. The miles to his bed, once covered in a single step, required a grueling march. Worry beset him. His pace picked up into a run. His ordeal ended in stumbling steps as he finally knocked on the doors of his home. Shock struck him as he realized the journey had taken too long. His home stood empty; his family gone.

*

She looked to the sky, but the sun refused to shine. The darkness surrounded her, cloaked her within a cold embrace. Despite the blackness, those eyes still watched her. They weren't normal eyes. Orbs, dried and withered long past their mortal life, watched her every move.

She could move away from them, but never be free of them. They were the sentries of a prison without walls. Sometimes she moved close to the boundary. Freedom seemed so enticingly close. Yet, the eyes silently watched her, daring her. Suddenly, the controlling, pitch black eyes called from the center of the prison.

"I see you, and you are mine. Bring me what I need, or stand in its place."

With no choice, she hunted the animal. It had been beautiful, wild and free, but now dead by her hands. She trudged it to the master. He took it from her, and bent its form. His will forced her to submit to her part in the transformation. He drew blood from her arm, using it for his magic. She witnessed the horror while enduring terror. The ceremony bestowed the creature the false life of an abomination. Its eyes dulled like the cold orbs of the other sentries. She had no doubt the same terror would one day befall her. Once he concluded his rite, he returned her to the darkness.

She would endure no more. "The way is open," she convinced herself.

Others worried for her safety: the living, warm eyes, with whom she shared the prison. She could not afford to lead them out as well. She had a feeling she would fail, and she would not have them suffer as she might. She ran for the wall-less boundary. There were gaps between the watching orbs, practically daring her to escape so she sprinted for it. When she got to the space between them, her body jerked to a stop. Invisible lines anchored her to the master. All she could do was scream and struggle, caught in the web.

*

He walked through the halls of his family's castle, looking through the eyes of his youth. His child legs ran playfully through stone halls of trophies and tapestries. The trimmings and decorations advertised his family's wealth. The halls stretched longer and chambers loomed larger than he recalled, but in his heart, he still knew this was home. Where were his brother and sister? Where was his family?

In a large chamber, he came to the throne overlooking the long dining table. It could easily host a score of guests, and often did. He moved towards it until a trophy, a boar's head mounted on the wall, looked right at him and arrested his movement. It seemed to glare at him. He turned, only to find another trophy watching him. This one stood as a full bear, but looked down on him as if ready to lay its claws on him. Even tapestry figures turned and stared at him.

"You don't belong here." A voice spoke. The child turned, seeing a stranger sitting tall and confidant upon his father's throne. No one had been sitting there a moment ago, and he couldn't clearly see the face. "Get out of my castle or I'll arrest you."

Scared, he turned to run. This was *his* home! Where was his family? What happened to their servants? The stranger behind him began shouting for the guards. More shouting. Thundering steps in the distance, approaching fast. Scared, he began running for the nearest exit yet he had trouble remembering exactly where to find it. He should know where the exit was, but every new room reminded him that it was at least one room farther. Armored boots clamored in chase. Hallways stretched and one junction lead to another. He couldn't find the door! The guards stamped closer, but he couldn't escape.

*

Laughter and good conversation surrounded the dreamer, as he enjoyed drinking the night away with his closest friends. He picked away a string of meat dangling from one of his tusks as he looked about the room through red eyes, physical traits he shared with everyone present. Their revelry this night would not be out-of-place among any race in the realm of Dhea Loral. A grand pavilion tent, made of stitched-together hides and supported by thick beams of wood, sheltered the partygoers as they danced around a bonfire. The tent stretched far enough that a hundred people could have slept within its warm embrace. Smoke from the bonfire flowed like mist around the occupants, before spiraling up through a hole near the center. Fur beds around the edges left revelers a place to rest. Many patrons gathered around a wall of kegs stacked to the ceiling. The crowd freely passed drinks around, one of which made its way to the dreamer. Caught up in the carousing, he danced his body through the crowd heedless of the foam spilling over the rim.

"Good times as ya ever see!" A friend clapped him on the shoulder.

He turned to agree, but stopped stiff with shock. A known friend stood there, laughing, a drink in one hand, patting him on the back with the other. Oddly enough, the friend also had an arrow stuck in his chest.

Unsure exactly how to react, he simply nodded and turned away. As long as his friend didn't mind the arrow, there was no need to break the mood of the moment. He moved into the crowd, joining several other friends in the words of a song.

One friend danced and appeared to sing, but the gash across his throat prevented the words from taking shape. Blood crusted the wound, but the reveler continued to clap hands and mouth the words. The dreamer's own song faltered as he witnessed the stricken dancer carry on.

Another called out, "You'll join us, won't you?"

He turned to the newest speaker. This friend, holding out a spare mug while standing amongst his own spilled entrails, said, "Your place is here."

Everyone standing around the speaker displayed mortal wounds. None seemed bothered by it and the party continued dancing and singing. The guests ignored their gashes, injuries, and escaping blood. More than one tried to put a hand out to him, offering him drinks.

He forced a friendly smile and turned away. Pretending nothing was amiss, he tried to put distance between himself and those stricken. He couldn't see any exits to the tent. He joined the singing just to calm his nerves as he pushed past more and more wounded friends looking for an escape. Every one of these friends should have been dead and buried. His song stuttered in nervous desperation as he tried pushing the hides at the side of the tent. Others kept laying hands on him, trying to pull him back.

"You belong with us," they insisted.

*

She looked up through the towering trees. A slight gap allowed the sun's rays to bask the forest floor upon which she stood. The sunlight silently invited her to reach up to it. She wanted to escape her grounded world, to fly in the wind alongside birds. A sudden fancy compelled her to try. She spread her arms, closed her eyes, and wished to touch the sky.

4

The wind wrapped about her, blowing her hair and making her feel weightless within her flapping robes. The ground fell away from her toes. She didn't open her eyes until a couple breaths had passed.

She was flying! Arms still outstretched, her body glided over the tops of the trees. Birds scattered, swarming about the sky around her. Her vision swept over her home city, looking at her neighbors as they looked back up at her. A smile split her face as her laughter echoed below.

In contrast, she noticed her people seemed scared. They pointed at the sky wearing frightened faces. Children screamed and ran. Guards rang alarm bells. People shouted to her, but the wind took their words.

Were they warning her? She looked about, finally spotting something that struck terror to her core. She saw a shadow cast across the trees below, large and malformed. The monstrous outline, hideous and fast, paced her. Fear kept her from looking up to see the owner. The birds weren't flocking for her, they were fleeing the creature. Similarly, her people fled the open clearings and ran for cover.

She tried to fly evasively. Her path veered left and right to avoid being an easy target. The shadow just grew larger, matching every movement. She couldn't even see her own slim shadow in order to gauge the distance.

The horrible truth dawned. The beastly shadow belonged to *her*.

Volume 1, Chapter 1   "The Regindals"

As his sword drew blood once again, he reflected on how little honor could be found in simply killing orcs. This didn't keep Archem Regindal, the field commander of his family and of their sworn vassals, from relishing the finishing blow to his opponent. He stepped back to measure the progress of his forces. The closest combatants surrounding him consisted of close family and the highest-ranking retainers. His bannerman stayed by his side as the standard of their family proclaimed control of this portion of the battlefield. Just ahead, a band of orcs continued to resist the line of advancing shields displaying the Regindal heraldry. The shields of the armsmen bore a red, two-headed griffin spreading its wings on a field of light blue. They marched as a wall, resplendent in similar colors.

Though the motley-garbed orcs fell back, Commander Archem felt as if something significant just happened, yet he failed to see the source. He glanced around, looking for his blood relatives. Archem's oldest son, named Hedgerdon III after one of their most famous ancestors, stood shoulder to shoulder with the armsmen as they advanced. He noticed his brother Marken, a warrior-priest of the goddess Dawn, waving an arm to get his attention.

"Did you feel the ground shake?" The armored priest shouted as he approached.

"I believe I did, where from?"

Marken directed Archem's eyes to the middle of the orc fortress. Rubble piled where a tower had stood only a minute before. The allied banners of Kashmer's army waved above the soldiers closest to the scene.

"The orcs retreated underground. They dropped the tunnel behind them."

"Another collapse?" Archem breathed a silent curse. It wouldn't do for a man of his stature to let unclean words pass openly. "Lady Jellaina! Attend!"

His eyes sought the woman. She bore a staff of arcane power, topped with a glowing crystal. Deep-blue robes displayed symbols only known to those schooled in magic. Jellaina and Archem were both beginning to lose their battle with gray hair; nevertheless, she rushed ahead of her apprentices as they maneuvered a small cart over fallen bodies. "Aye, cousin?"

Archem indicated the motley last-stand of orcs pressed against the inside of the outer wall by their retainers. "End that resistance now!"

"And take the glory from your son?"

Hedgerdon III could be seen stabbing his latest victim. Armsmen next to him cheered as they tried to copy his success. Archem stood taller and his chest swelled watching his heir's actions.

"He will understand. More glory awaits us underground."

Both of his kin reflected momentary confusion. Archem continued, "Their hostage must be in warrens under this fort. Down there, we will claim the glory of the campaign."

Jellaina directed her apprentices. As one, they began spellcasting. Within moments, a firestorm along the wall immolated the remaining resistance. Meanwhile, the warrior-priest called on his own acolytes to dispense healing miracles to their fallen. Marken then fell into pace behind Commander Archem, striding together toward the rubble. All resistance from that portion of the fort had ended. Kashmer's Army paused to regroup, milling uncertainly about the closed tunnel.

Marken asked, "How do you intend to follow them below ground?"

Archem borrowed a downed orc's cloak to wipe his sword, returning it to the scabbard. "I will call on Djizzoud's second favor."

"Hmphf! Kashmer is only offering a speck of land outside the gates as a reward. We are paying more than we gain."

Archem grinned, "In gold value, aye."

Priest Marken didn't immediately respond, readjusting his golden-sun holy symbol of Dawn. Archem noticed the movement. He had once asked how the Goddess of Life and Rebirth favored Marken's warrior ways. Marken had answered that Dawn favored the conflicts and chaos of life to bring strength to the survivors.

By the time Archem spoke again, Jellaina and Hedgerdon III rejoined them. "Rarely do we have such opportunity to impress the folk of Kashmer directly. Much of our work exploring and fighting are done away from the population. Today, we will show the common man such prestige and resourcefulness that they will be talking of it in the taverns for centuries. Let the Kashmer commanders know we are calling in Djizzoud. We don't want our allies panicking or causing an incident when they see an elemental prince appear."

Jellaina's arched eyebrow spoke volumes, but she moved to make ready. Her apprentices manhandled the cart of arcane resources over more bodies as they approached. The lady wizard retrieved an ornate statue from a drawer within it. The design imitated a humanoid creature of stone, holding aloft one oversized hand. The hand had the thumb and little finger tucked across the palm, extending two of the other three fingers upward. The third finger, once extended, ended where someone once broke it.

"Lord Archem, they may disapprove." Jellaina commented.

Marken Regindal walked towards them, flanked by three Kashmer officers.

"We best get this done before we find out."

Archem reached for the statue and snapped one of the remaining fingers. Jellaina blushed at the remaining upraised finger adorning the statue. Hedgerdon III stifled a laugh.

Thunder without lightening cracked across the sky. The ground shifted. Soldiers of the city of Kashmer backed away as a large hand reached up from solid ground. An arm and a head soon followed. The ground seemed to melt upward and bind with the ascending giant. Stone slabs, piles of rocks, and the top layer of dirt helped form the body. His black-jewel eyes glanced around, forcing warriors to recoil as they viewed those bottomless depths. He towered twenty feet over the members of the Regindal family, yet he stopped rising a short distance below where the beltline would be. His size and composition panicked several soldiers. The Regindal family and most of their retainers stood firm.

The behemoth's words rumbled across the ground like an aftershock. "What do you request?"

Archem indicated the collapsed tower, calling for the removal of rubble and access to the tunnels underneath. Djizzoud's mouth, ringed with the former rock slabs of the orc fortress, smirked. "Such a pitifully easy task. This will be your family's second favor. Upon the request of your third, the rest of your payment is due."

Jellaina and Marken cast a worried look at Archem, but he didn't reconsider. "Proceed," he called.

The titan's upper torso slid across the ground. Digging in with both monstrous hands, it began gouging the earth under the rubble. The ground didn't resist. In the upheaval, he threw aside boulders weighing tons.

Archem put a hand on his son's shoulder. "Reassemble the armsmen into a charge formation. As soon as the way opens, Jellaina will use fire, then we rush in. I want us inside before the city's regulars can properly form up."

Hedgerdon III cast a look at the regular army. The soldiers alongside them were Kashmer's elite. The trade city, home to the largest merchant fleet in the world as well as the Regindal family, had sent their best soldiers along with a wave of privateers deep into the orc hills. The navy's strength and resources ranked the highest in the known world. It protected the real ruling class of Kashmer: the fat purses of the merchant guilds. The city's proud army eagerly sought to win their own renown.

However, the noble Regindal family had spent a ridiculous amount of gold and expendable magic to pave the way ahead of everyone. Kashmer's populace looked up to the family as legends. They would not let their pride be stung by falling short of their goal just outside their hometown, or by letting common soldiers get ahead of them.

The Kashmer soldiers stood awestruck in the face of the titan's display. A few cowered or retreated from the rain of large stones. The nobles noted how several soldiers in the back began talking excitedly. No doubt, Archem's words would prove correct. This event would be replayed in Kashmer taverns for centuries.

The elemental prince Djizzoud threw aside the last slab of stone. Archem knew the way was clear as he heard the surprised orc screams from below. A few feeble arrows launched out of the hole, wasted on the hard exterior of the djinn. The noble family's armsmen marched to the titan's side as the rest of the army still cowered.

"Second favor, granted. I look forward to our third meeting." As the words left it, the rocky djinn melted back into the stones.

Jellaina led her apprentices behind the shelter of the armsmen's shields. They set off a series of rehearsed, and perfectly timed spells. The first spells detonated the orcs in direct line of sight from the forced entry. The next attacks rolled into the tunnel system and followed the halls until they found a target. Fiery explosions caused shimmering heat waves to roll out from the hole.

Archem instructed his bannerman to wave the family flag proudly. He called out the family's motto to embolden them: "As Kashmer ventures, the Regindals must lead!"

"Dawn's rejuvenation shines upon you, her children." Marken spoke at the completion of a prayer. The miracle-infused benediction fell upon the surrounding troops, granting them an unseen but palpable physical enhancement. Skin hardened and muscles thickened.

Bolstered by the inspiration of their Lord Archem and the divine aid of Marken, Hedgerdon III and the armsmen rolled forward. Every soldier in their retinue had a specific job in which he excelled. As they breached the orc tunnels they displayed their worth. The Regindal family liked to think of themselves as professionals rather than adventurers, holding themselves to a high standard of planning and performance. Tricks were used to set off any traps from a distance. Archers and apprentice wizards among the armsmen took out orc assassins before they got close. When a wild melee of orcs would charge in, the shield ranks of armsmen executed practiced moves as a unit. Their steel-toed boots marched over the mangled remains of their enemies.

The expanded network of tunnels forced the house retainers to divide down multiplying halls. Archem directed them, "We must figure out where they hold Lord Felnick. They will be offering the most resistance in the halls leading to their captive."

As reports filtered from runners, Archem believed he understood which route held the most importance. As progress slowed, and Marken warned him of the danger to his extended forces, an archer confirmed a sighting. As Archem's closest family fought valiantly through another chamber, the cornered orcs offered increasingly desperate fights. At the far end of the newly conquered chamber, the Regindals paused to reassess their situation.

Aside from Archem, Jellaina, Marken and Hedgerdon III, only a handful of retainers defended the nobles. The rest were strewn in a jagged line extending back to the surface. As runners came and went, Lord Archem began to piece the layout of the tunnels and resistance in his mind. His face lit with a smile after listening to the latest messenger.

The lord proclaimed for everyone in the room, "This is the group! We've got them trapped!" Pointing to the runner, he instructed, "Tell the others to use their last spells if needed, but *hold those tunnels*! We can't leave them an escape."

The runner sprinted away. Jellaina saw the eagerness in Archem's face and couldn't resist a smile. "Like older times, cousins. This will come down to us." Her glance included Marken as well, for they had shared many adventures during their youth.

Before they could advance, a voice called from ahead. By its guttural accent, its orc origin sounded clear. "Stop! Nay killing! We 'ave your mewlin' lord; offer trade!"

Lord Archem agreed with his cousin's sentiment. The results of this encounter sat squarely on their shoulders, without much retainer support. He actually relished the idea. He perused a handful of past strategies in his head. His hand sought the comfort of his sword handle.

Archem glanced at Jellaina, "Do you still have that trick bracelet?"

Her face paled, "Aye, though I dread using it."

*

The Regindal family walked with weapons in hand, venturing into a large chamber. Stolen tapestries and untidy stacks of treasure decorated this throne room. The stink of sweat and blood mixed with burning incense saturated the enclosed area. The orc-chieftain wasn't hard to miss. Archem assumed it was the gaudy orc, dressed in feather plumes and wearing multiple jeweled necklaces, holding a knife at the throat of a human in formerly fine garments. The lord's stained dress reflected the poor treatment he'd been given; it even matched the gagging stench of the room. He watched the Regindals' approach with a hint of relief in his eyes. He said nothing, however, perhaps due to the jagged blade hovering just under his jaw.

The noble adventurers took stock of the room. The circular chamber spread nearly twenty meters in diameter. Light came from lit braziers surrounding an idol. The golden figure, bearing exaggerated orc features, likely consisted of melted goods from centuries of raided Kashmer caravans. A number of wooden supports braced the ceiling, doubling as cover for half a dozen orc archers. Another four warriors flanked the closest entry, hands holding weapons. An orc standing near the apparent chieftain wore bits of animal trophies, displayed a painted face, and held a pinch of colored dirt in his hand as he muttered gibberish. Mystic or shaman, the Regindals knew he would be one of the biggest threats. Two other exits could be seen across the room. More orcs could be seen beyond those doorways.

The far orcs paid little attention to the humans entering the main chamber. Archem could hear sounds of fighting beyond the far end. This puzzled him. The Regindal retainers flanking to cut off any escape wouldn't have been able to access the tunnels from that side.

"I make the offers in this place," the chieftain spoke. "You have caused too much death over one hostage."

"We don't like to encourage kidnappings," Archem replied. He planned to say more, but the chief interrupted.

"He walked our lands! Hunted our meat supply! You will accept my demand, leave tribute as you go, and we will release him once your armies are out of the hills."

"Leave tribute?" Archem gave a side glance at Jellaina. "I thought we made it clear by this invasion, Kashmer won't pay. We'll be happy to leave your lives and homes intact if you hand him over now. You are not in a position of strength."

The orc leader yanked on Lord Felnick's hair, flicking his knife up to scratch the chin. "Deceiving yourself? I have the power here!"

A voice roared out from one of the far tunnels. It was far enough away as to barely be heard, but they made out the words, "Feel Nandorrin's fury!" A hiss of flames could be seen and heard from one of the far tunnels. The chieftain and his shaman glanced over their shoulders. The gout of flames backlit a few orcs in the far tunnel, staggering to get out of the way.

The words puzzled Archem. Nandorrin was a god worshipped by dwarves. Did the orcs have a dwarf prisoner too? Was he loose and causing problems? Regardless, the distraction offered the best opportunity for Jellaina's trick.

Archem glanced over to Jellaina. His firm nod conveyed his meaning. Jellaina sucked in a breath as she prepared herself for the worst. Her hands had been clasped in a relaxed manner against the front of her belt. One hand grabbed and twisted a gem on her magic bracelet.

Most sounds ceased. The rest became a deep, slow baritone as she moved into action. Everyone, orcs and family members alike, stood frozen in time. One of her hands rose, beginning a nimble dance of patterns that would release spell energy. Her other hand drew forth a wickedly sharp and curved dagger from her belt. The spell completed. Just ahead of her hands, a white ball began to materialize in midair.

Spending no more thought on it, she slashed the necks of both armed orcs standing over her. The blade passed under their chins with minimal resistance. Both orcs continued to snarl and stare…still unaware of the movement of the wizard, much less the fact that she'd already delivered their death.

Jellaina Regindal began a sprint towards the chieftain. Her free hand began twisting around the contortions of a second spell. As yet, no one else seemed to move at all, but she knew time would resume soon, and then she'd be vulnerable. Her hand finished the gestures and she spoke a word of power. Three spectral arrows appeared. They floated about her free hand, awaiting orders. She pointed at the head of one orc archer. The first arrow launched on its journey, but moved slower than she did.

She was careful to step around the glowing white sphere created by her first spell. Only now did it show signs of moving forward.

Another step or two would bring her to the orc chieftain. She paused as another target came into view. Jellaina pointed a second time, sending the second arrow crawling across the air toward another orc.

The chieftain was within reach. His gaze still half-turned to the gout of flames still visible across the chamber, beyond the far door. The orcs in the next room seemed to be on a stairwell, looking downward at the source of the fire. They paid no attention to the action in the chieftain's room. Disregarding the spectacle, Jellaina used her dagger and tore a line across his throat easily.

The pitch of the sounds began to change. An almost imperceptible movement came from both chieftain and noble as they still responded to the earlier distraction. She had to remove the threatening dagger from the lord's throat, or the orc might still be able to kill the man. Her free hand grabbed at the knife and attempted to yank it loose. Unfortunately, the attempt wasn't succeeding as fast as she'd hoped. The knife slowly turned away, but she couldn't pull it from his grasp. Instead she retracted the dagger and drove it into the chieftain's arm. Hopefully, that would make him lose his grip.

The shaman was almost within reach. She pointed her free hand. The third and last arrow left her hand's side, needing to cross only two feet of distance before it would transfix his brain.

The white, glowing ball accelerated its flight alongside the wizard. It moved faster than she did. Jellaina turned to flee for the safety of her kin. In doing so, she realized another orc archer, bow drawn and ready, stood between her and the entry. Its hand visibly drew back the bowstring. No surprise, since its brain was beginning to register the geysers of blood erupting from the first two orcs she had slashed. Its arrow pointed directly at Archem even as the lord leaned forward to charge the enemy.

She knew she would not pass him in time, so she dove at the back of his legs. It was a desperate act. The reason she hated using the bracelet was that the device carried a slight curse. Soon, the bubble of time that accelerated her would even things out by slowing her down. A vulnerable and time-stopped Jellaina would be an easy kill for any orcs left to threaten her. As she crashed into the archer's legs, the orc almost seemed to be moving as fast as she was.

As time accelerated everyone around her, she caught one horrifying sight. Another orc, hidden by the idol, had been looking in the direction of his leader. In his upraised hand, he held a dagger ready for the throw. The orc, seeing his leader attacked and the woman responsible, flung it at her. Time accelerated the movement, while Jellaina paused in slow motion with wide eyes and a silent scream upon her lips.

Archem's head barely returned forward as he felt the splash of orc blood to one side of his face. He charged straight forward, planning to get near the hostage in case Jellaina could not neutralize all the threats.

His mind registered a blur of motion directly ahead, without being able to track her movements.

The orc chieftain screamed and staggered, knife clattering against the floor. Lord Felnick rolled for cover…the wrong way…even as the shaman dropped dead from a magical arrow sticking out of his head.

A white sphere flew to the far end of the room. The comet exploded, sending icicle shards into all the archers taking cover in that area. Another pair of orcs fell from hiding, similarly pierced by glowing arrows. Marken and Hedgerdon III attacked the two orcs standing opposite the ones Jellaina slashed.

In his rush, Archem almost missed seeing the orc archer hiding directly ahead. The archer shook as something or someone hit him from behind. The arrow whistled harmlessly over his shoulder. The collision gave Lord Archem the opening he needed to easily run his sword through the archer. He retracted his weapon immediately, searching for the next target.

A flash of motion caught his eyes. It came from the idol and struck near the archer's legs. Jellaina! Time froze her diving body in place. A dagger hilt protruded from her torso! Archem turned his wrath in the direction of the throw. The orc hiding there barely managed to draw a second dagger before Archem's sword chop lopped the orc a foot shorter from the top.

"Marken! Jellaina is struck!"

Archem quickly glanced around the room. None of the orcs still stood. Lord Felnick seemed alright. The lord shakily got to his hands and knees. Several of the remaining Regindal retainers charged into the room.

"Secure the exits!" Lord Archem directed.

His men jumped to obey. Archem turned his attention to his cousin. Jellaina was beginning to catch up to time. Noise escaped her shocked mouth as she started to reflexively curl around her wound. Marken didn't wait for time to speed up. The warrior-priest yanked the dagger out. Jellaina's blood sluggishly oozed forward. The priest spoke his healing prayer, channeling the divine power of his goddess. The miracle sealed the wound even as the Regindals' wizard caught up to real time.

"Aaaaahh! Nirahha's Face! I hate using that bracelet!" Jellaina swore.

As she continued to curse, Marken winked at Archem. "She'll be fine. The time flux kept her from bleeding much by the time I could heal her."

With relief, Lord Archem stood and moved to properly greet the orcs' former prisoner. "Lord Felnick. It is my privilege to see you well. Have you been harmed?"

"Mostly in pride," he replied, shrugging off visible pain as any highborn noble of Kashmer would be expected to do. His next words were more revealing, "Though if you can spare the services, they have given me a bruise or two. You are Regindals, I expect?"

Lord Archem drew himself to full stature with pride. "We are, and proud to assist! Priest Marken?"

Dawn's priest finished helping Jellaina to her feet. The wizard stood somewhat stooped, clutching at what was likely just ghost pain remaining from the wound. Convinced she would be fine, Marken hurried to Lord Felnick's side.

A resonating boom left a slight tremor in the floor.

A chorus of questions erupted from the group as they looked about. One of the armsmen from the far exit called out for their attention. Beyond him, a battle yet raged. Several armsmen and a few of Jellaina's acolytes engaged a group of orcs in the next room. The orcs were at a lower elevation than the idol room, making it difficult to see. Since Lord Archem assisted their noble guest, Hedgerdon III rushed to oversee the situation. He returned even as a second loud boom shook dust from the walls.

Marken attended Lord Felnick's wounds as Hedgerdon III pulled his father aside. "A stairway in the next room descends into a large chamber. Some dead orcs lie near a closed double-door at the bottom. Dozens of living orcs are either trying to ascend the stairs against our forces, or use a battering ram to gain entry to a room underneath this one."

His words were punctuated by repetitive impacts from the next room. Archem briefly weighed his curiosity before discarding the idea. He addressed his family and armsmen. "We have rescued our goal. Let us see him safely to the surface. Withdraw in good order and proud bearing."

Before he had advanced two steps, Lord Felnick paused. "My possessions! Precious heirlooms!" At seeing the frowns from some of the armsmen, he indicated the chieftain. "It's in the room here, he has the key."

The noble pulled a key from the corpse and stepped away from the others. A solid chest could be seen in the back of the room. A few clicks, and the noble began pulling shiny objects from it and stuffing his pockets. The Regindal family paid him little heed, turning their attention to reorganizing their retainers.

A resounding crash overpowered all other noise. Lord Archem had no doubt that the doors in the room below had just fallen, but to what end? Orc war cries roared with renewed fire. Archem turned to face the noble. "Your lordship…"

Lord Felnick Pentle looked up from the chest, kneeling alone on that side of the room. He perked up at the presumed danger and rose.

Two unfamiliar voices cried out in common, barely heard as they mixed in with the orc war cries from below. "First Hand!" and "Dalios count you!"

Everyone looked about in confusion as the roars belonging to multiple beasts met against the threats of the orcs. A rumble shook the floor of the room. Sharp cracks in the stone reverberated in the small space. Lord Archem Regindal helplessly watched as the floor of the room began collapsing from one end to the other. A rolling wave cracked the floor before dropping it into the unknown. Lord Felnick, standing alone, barely had time to let his eyes go wide before the calamity rolled under his feet and swallowed him. In moments, stones crashing from both floor and ceiling left a great pit taking up half the room. Tiny shafts of sunlight speared through the dustcloud. Archem stumbled, poised on the edge of his own doom. A hand, Hedgerdon III perhaps, grabbed his cloak and pulled him back a few steps. The orc war cries disappeared. The animal-like noises continued onward, carried away into echoes. The Regindals dumbly stared at the edge of the pit into which their prestige and glory had fallen.

Lord Archem summoned up the courage to run to the edge, heedless of any remaining danger. Dust rolled up from the pit, concealing its secrets for several anxious moments. Casting his eyes on the unveiling catastrophe below, he exclaimed, "What devilry was this?"

Volume 1, Chapter 2   **"Drawing Lots"**

Sails remained furled as a diverse congregation of races and professions milled about the deck. Men with travel-stained robes stood beside bearded knights. Elf archers distanced themselves from a retinue of dwarves. A feral-looking woman wearing animal skins peered over the shoulder of a robed man, scrunching her eyes as she tried to read the odd writing on the scroll in his hands. Amidst the crowded deck, folk managed to find a means to give room to a short but broad-shouldered half-orc. They kept distance as he applied war paint to his face using the blood of a seagull he managed to catch. One young woman sat upon a yardarm after using magical flight, preferring her vantage above the crowd, despite repeated calls from the sailors to get down. One unfortunate member of the domid race, short-statured people normally renowned for their endless appetite, expelled his breakfast over the side though anchors still moored the ship in the calm harbor. Brute or frail, armored or bared, different races…a commonality forced them together on the deck of the ship.

The sound of stomping footsteps carried over the noise of the crowd. People paused to turn their attention to the scarred old salt ascending to the forecastle. Voices hushed at his presence. The man wore the colors and insignias of an officer in the Kashmer Navy. He turned at the top rail to address the crowd, but his gaze focused on the lone yardarm sitter.

"Get down on the deck now, or be knocked down hard."

His voice rolled with authority across the deck, and a number of uniformed sailors stepped up beside him. The young woman noted the seriousness and promptly floated back down.

"You are onboard *Lancer*, veteran galleon of the Kashmer Navy," he continued, his eyes scanning the crowd with clear disdain. "I am First Mate Vanford. Let's be brief and to the point. You are here because you are all privateers, contracted to protect Kashmer and her holdings. Your skills are required to aid our kingdom, for we have an urgent need. Kashmer thanks you for her service."

A few mutterings came from scattered voices in the crowd, most too low for the First Mate to make out individual words.

"I wasn't asked here, I was forced."

"Second time in a year they've pressed us into service."

"Nay, last year they asked for volunteers for the Stonelands, this time we're *told* we're going."

"For some noble scat as well. Pitiful emergency!"

The first mate grabbed a belaying pin from its holder and rapped it hard against the railing. The dissension subsided almost immediately. "You've all signed the new contracts for your privateer service to Kashmer this year; we *can* conscript you for urgent matters concerning the kingdom. But we are not without offering recompense. All of you will receive payment for your time. The individual or group most responsible for rescuing Lord Pentle will receive a land grant, free of levies for ten years, on a prime spot on the east trade road, just outside the main gate."

"The Lord Mayor?" someone shouted.

Vanford rolled his eyes. "Lord *Felnick* Pentle, seventh in line to the throne of Kashmer, and nephew to our Lord Mayor: Duke Havnor Pentle. Captured by orcs in the southern hills while out hunting. We know he's alive, but the ransom demanded by the orcs is unrealistic. The armies of Kashmer need you to bolster our numbers as we venture into the hills for a rescue."

"Someone must prefer war over the poor lordling," a dwarf priest bearing a flame-pattern shield hmphed to those around him. "This will surely get him killed."

"…the main force of our army is striking south of the trade route in the area the lord was hunting." Vanford continued. "The navy, including all of you, is landing on the shores west of the area and pushing into the hills from there."

The first mate pointed to the deck below his vantage, indicating a table holding five different colored buckets. "We learned in the Stonelands that privateers work better in small squads. You will approach the table below. If you are already part of a group, register there. If not, pick a numbered tile from an appropriately colored bucket. The number will be your squad. Front-line warriors pick from the red tiles, those with healing magic pick from the blue…"

*

Pondering the numbered, red tile in one gauntleted hand, Sir Cruso Lanvyrl smoothed out his thick mustache and neatly trimmed beard with his other hand. He used this last chance to look his best for whatever new friends, or enemies, he was about to meet. At six feet, two inches, he had a good view over most of the crowd. With the abundance of weapons and armor he wore, he also had the fortune that most people moved out of his way. In contrast to his tough exterior, he issued a steady stream of "pardon me" and "thank you" as he moved.

Everyone shouted numbers in an attempt to link up with their lots. Groups began forming across the deck, though it remained crowded between individuals.

After calling out "eighteen" for what seemed like as many times, he heard a voice answer, "Over here!"

Cruso's attention was drawn to a pair of women leaning against some barrels. The speaker, also human, still had her arm upraised. Her accent and brown skin set her apart, a noticeably darker shade than any native of the continent of Quoros. Her endowed curves could turn many men's heads. Despite this, the other female captured Cruso's attention. He recalled seeing her once before.

In contrast to her companion's dark beauty, a female elf with pale skin and long, blonde hair, regarded him as he approached. Her brightly colored clothing stood out amongst the gathered rabble. Recognizing her from a prior encounter only a few days earlier, his eyes riveted longer than may have been polite. The elf's eyes narrowed slightly. Maybe subconsciously, she stepped one leg back. Noticing it, Cruso wondered if she still had bandages underneath her robe. She broke the stare, returning her attention to the yellow tile in her hand. Yellow…magic-user.

Her lack of friendliness now and the earlier time he had seen her, despite never trading a word, made him feel awkward. He turned his attention to the dark-skinned woman instead. He approached and offered a respective bow, stretching left leg back, left hand over heart, and a right-hand flourish.

"Now we have everyone, even Diaran royalty," someone muttered in the crowd nearby. Cruso had forgotten that in these barbaric lands, sometimes a 'bow' consisted of simply a head nod, though he found it disrespectful.

Displaying the red tile inscribed with eighteen, he said, "Good tidings, fair ladies. I am Sir Cruso Lanvyrl, at your service."

The dusky human seemed taken back, unsure how to respond. "I…uh…Vallese. Good day."

"Nay surname?" he asked. Vallese tilted her head to the side, looking confused. Cruso didn't recognize her accent, and wondered if she couldn't understand all his words. He continued, "A family name? Or possibly a title?"

"Maybe she prefers a little privacy. Many folk go by one name." The elf's voice flowed smoothly. Her speech intoned in such a way that she didn't seem to be rebuking Cruso's possible social blunder. "I am Allisee Lentara. I recall seeing you two nights ago."

Cruso's eyes flitted to Allisee's leg, but this was a new outfit she wore, hiding the injury that he knew lie hidden. Returning his gaze fully to her cerulean eyes, he said, "I apologize if I offended you by staring that day. You seemed…out of place."

"I have a feeling we both appeared out of place." This time, Cruso felt rebuked, yet the elf managed it in the sweetest possible tone. The flow of her voice matched the rest of her beauty. "But what did you expect? Someone to trade war stories? Compare who had the biggest scar?"

As Cruso stumbled for a response, Vallese asked, in her odd accent, "I am missing something?"

Cruso started to open his mouth, but glanced sideways to see Allisee's response as she said, "Please, share." Her tone didn't indicate whether her eyes would judge him by how he shared the account.

The knight began his tale. "I am new here to Kashmer. In looking to set a new start for myself, I got involved in a fight. I hoped to help someone in danger. It didn't go as perfectly as I had planned. When it was over, I needed a proper divine healer to tend my wounds.

"This took me to the Monastery of The Codex. A monk escorted me through the temple to a place where they could channel their healing energies. That monastery is also the only public library in Kashmer. We passed rows of shelves filled with tomes and scrolls. My gaze was drawn to the only other visitor there who didn't look like a monk."

Cruso's attention shifted from Vallese to the elf. "If you don't mind me saying, Allisee, your elven features and striking dress appeared quite different from the normal fashion of that place. You sat there, frowning, puzzling over a written script. You had quill and ink at the ready. I couldn't help but notice the leg you rested upon a stool. The dress torn and stained bandages covering a leg wound not fully healed. It is in my nature to feel defensive of such a fair person who had suffered such injuries. My inquisitiveness got the best of me. I believe I stared, trying to guess at your mystery."

Cruso glanced down to the deck. "Your gaze noticed mine, and a slight glare from you gave all the warning I needed. I know when not to ask questions. So I stepped by to receive the healing for my own wounds. You were still sitting there on my way out. Same pose, bandaged leg supported. I kept my eyes to my feet as I walked, respecting your privacy." He paused to take a deep breath. "Perhaps we should speak no more of the past, for our future has more pressing matters."

His tale ended as he noticed two others standing nearby. The first of the two, a young, wiry woman, introduced herself as Eryn. The second, the owner of a very boisterous voice, announced his presence as Yedrak, faithful champion of Dalios. The man looked every inch of his calling as a priest honoring the God of War and Strength. He carried more weapons than Cruso, and cruel spikes adorned his armor.

"We're being formed in groups of five," reasoned Cruso, as he watched the other groups forming and the mix of tiles displayed.

"So, we're full?" Vallese questioned.

*

The inquiry, spoken in her unusual accent, caught a wandering ear. Her voice and inflection sounded familiar to the broad-shouldered half-orc, his face war-painted by the blood of the dead seagull. He noticed Vallese and her four groupmates standing together, before glancing at the tile in his hand: number six black. He raised his eyes to reconsider the individuals of the group. The half-orc looked over the armaments of Cruso and Yedrak, knowing immediately neither would be carrying the black tile for their group. His eyes, red irises on yellow orbs, studied Allisee. He muttered, "And yer a yella-tiled finger wiggler if I've ever seen 'un."

His gaze darted between the curvaceous, dusk-skinned woman and the wiry female next to her. The darker woman held an unstrung bow in her hands, along with a sturdy staff. The other carried only daggers…lots of them. He knew one of them from a brief encounter, but tried to recall her name.

"Vallese? Yer the long-distance expert…" The orc-blood muttered to himself, glanced at his black tile before his eyes returned to the wiry female carrying all the daggers. "So ya must be the scout."

He walked up to the group. "Hello, Vallese. Ya really are explorin' the worst parts of Kashmer."

She turned to him, eyes widening in surprise. He assumed his warpaint caused her to gasp and take a step backward. Of course, that was just one of the benefits of a good covering of warpaint; humans seemed to cower from it. It amazed him that this woman shunned such décor. Her arms were covered with old scratches. A spotted tattoo pattern covered her bared shoulders and ringed her ankles. The marks gave her skin more character than most humans.

She found her voice after a brief pause. "Hello…Urtusk?"

"Ha-ra, Ha-ra!" He bellowed and repeated several times, drawing attention from others along the deck. It took the others a few moments to understand it as laughter. "I can see where ya'd make that mistake." He ran a finger along one of a pair of tusks that originated from his jaw and curved over some of his upper lip. "Urgosk."

"Oh. Sorry."

"Still don't talk much, do ya?" Urgosk didn't wait for a reply. He turned his attention to Eryn, holding up his number six black tile. "We're switchin' groups."

Eryn unconsciously clenched the dark shape in her hands. "What? Why would I do that!?"

Urgosk turned to the knightly figure. "Are you the high-bred Diaran everyone here thinks you are?"

The knight went rigid. Had the orc overheard the comment during the earlier bow? He had to admit, his armor and the coat of arms on his shield may look ostentatious compared to most of the privateers. "I am Sir Cruso, and it may amuse you to know I *do* belong to a respected house in Diara. But…"

Urgosk interrupted, swinging his gaze back to Eryn. "Haughty, isn't he? Now that ye've seen yer group's prospects, take a looksie over at my group." Urgosk pointed to a group of men milling about the mainsail. "There stands a promising young mage with a full purse. Oh, and the famed Khepov brothers, ye heard of 'em?"

Eryn looked down his pointing arm, her eyes going wide as she saw the two handsome brothers. Both were becoming legends among Kashmer's Privateers, mostly for prowess and showmanship in the arena. She nodded, her mouth slightly agape. Urgosk added, "And both are still looking for the right young lass."

With barely a look back at the others, Eryn traded tiles. "Good luck!" She walked away.

Urgosk flashed the number 18 black tile at Vallese with a tusk-gated smile. "Looks like I get to be yer guide again." The armored priest of Dalios, Yedrak, hadn't said much as he observed the exchange. The big man crossed his arms as he stared down at Urgosk. The half-orc could see the distrust upon his visage.

The elf magic-weaver spoke up, "You know the Khepov brothers?"

Urgosk turned to her. "Nay, we just met. They bragged about their arena wins. And yer…"

"Allisee." She leaned closer to the orc. Urgosk stood clearly as the more imposing, due to his solid, muscular frame and the large battleaxe carried in one hand. However, Allisee had the advantage of a couple inches in height. She looked down in order to talk to him. "So, within a couple minutes of meeting two gladiator brothers, strangers to you, on a ship bound to slay orcs, you found out whether they were courting or not?"

Urgosk's toothy smile returned, "Nay, of course not. I just figger'd I had good odds that one of them would be free. Or, simply willing to bed a girl before a big fight."

"Is that what *you* seek?" Vallese asked, with a firm grip on her quarterstaff.

Urgosk smirked, "Only if she talks me out of my knightly vows." At which he made a point of glancing at Cruso's reddened face.

Allisee decided to calm the situation. She had no intention of going into someone else's war with a group that boiled each other's kettles. "You obviously know each other. I'd like to hear that tale." She glanced back and forth between Urgosk and Vallese.

Vallese looked uncomfortable being the focus of the group. Urgosk, who seemed to have a smirk or a tusk-gated smile, gave her time to volunteer before opening his mouth to speak. Yedrak seemed to be staring a spear straight to his heart. The priest obviously didn't trust him. Maybe prejudiced?

The orc-blood began his tale. "I'm half-human, though I've lived my life with my orc tribe. It came time to find a new home, and all ships seem to pass through Kashmer. I've actually been here a few months. Jobs are hard to find for one of my looks, unless you know where to go.

One of those jobs has been at Yetrayal's Hold…the gambling house here on the docks. They keep me topped off."

Urgosk hooked a finger on one of the many necklaces he wore, revealing a flask just underneath his stained tunic.

"I also appreciate fine vintage in humans, and while at the docks I spot this curvy beauty walkin' off a boat. New arrival. Vallese looked overwhelmed. Her eyes were everywhere, I was surprised she didn't fall off the dock. Could tell she never saw Kashmer b'fore. Needless to say, her armor caught my eyes."

Urgosk motioned to the armor Vallese currently wore. The others took a fresh look, though Sir Cruso only took a brief glance before averting his eyes.

Upon seeing their reactions, Vallese snapped, "What is wrong with this armor?"

"It is quite lewd," Yedrak's boisterous voice carried across the deck. Allisee jumped, having almost forgotten the big man standing so quietly next to her.

Sir Cruso, staring slightly away from Vallese out of respect, stated, "It leaves many openings. It lacks the mettle for war."

Vallese shook her head. "I didn't want metal, too heavy. Leather is more to my comfort."

As Cruso pondered the misunderstanding with a slack-jawed mouth, Allisee asked, "Where did you get it?"

"Archer's Port."

"The pirate port?" Yedrak asked.

"Ha-ra, ha-ra," Urgosk laughed as he continued. "That explains it. They deal more in slaves, luxuries, and good looks. I think you walked into the wrong 'armory' down there."

Urgosk brazenly looked over Vallese's figure. "Anyway, you seemed lost on the docks. Eyes up and down the street were watching your swinging purse, as well as the gem pouch at your neck. It was a matter of time before one tried his luck, and I made sure I was there when they did." Urgosk raised his arms and cracked his knuckles together. "Vallese's reflexes are good. She slapped the hand that cut her purse string, but then the thief ripped free her gem pouch. She didn't know what to do. Her coin purse hit the dockside as the thief ran with the other pouch, but I caught him."

"The orc…half-orc…is fast. Runs like wind." Vallese interrupted. "Bent thief's arm where it shouldn't bend."

"Goods saved. I was her noble knight!" Urgosk smirked at Sir Cruso, but addressed Vallese. "How many gems did I save?"

Vallese's hand went to the small pouch at her neck. "Not gems. Other items."

"Valuable?"

"To me. Junk to others."

"Ah, well, after that we introduced ourselves and I offered to give her a tour of Kashmer. It didn't last long."

Vallese huffed, "You were more interested in finding bed to share. Molly helped me just fine, and at less cost!"

"Molly?" Inquired Allisee.

Urgosk shrugged, "A street rat."

Seeing the others' uncomprehending glances, the elf provided, "Kashmer has a number of orphans. Many of them line up at the gates or docks to play tour guides for a cheap price."

"Ah, but now fate thrusts us together again," Urgosk proclaimed to Vallese.

*

No sooner had Urgosk proclaimed the reunion by fate, a dwarf stomping through the crowd of privateers looked around at the group. He spotted Sir Cruso and quickly ran his eyes across the others. Noting the balance of the group tilted towards warrior-types, the dwarf came to a decision and said, "Fate's reunion, indeed."

The dwarf's eyes stayed on Sir Cruso for an extended time, until the knight realized he was being watched. Cruso squinted at the dwarf for a moment before uttering, "Heavyboot?"

As the others turned to follow Cruso's gaze, the dwarf stepped forward. "Aye, you remember. Mornik Heavyboot, priest of Nandorrin, at your service." The dwarf offered a bow that left his beard dipping past his knees.

"Another priest?" Yedrak asked, holding aloft the blue tile in his hand.

The dwarf turned to the newest speaker. "And I recognize you as a chosen of Dalios, are you not?" At that, Yedrak puffed up taller and broader in stature. Mornik nodded and continued. "I thought you might be willing to trade groups."

"You doubt my abilities here?"

"Nay, just the opposite. I feel you may benefit my group more. Our 'red tile' is a duelist, wielding a thin poker. Almost all of them have some magic abilities, but wouldn't be great going toe-to-toe with a rush of orcs." Mornik hefted his hammer, indicating it. The hammer's head featured tiny rows of spikes, but also tapered into a long spike on the back end. "Although I love smashing opponents with Heel here, Nandorrin grants me fire magic to smote foes."

The dwarf priest gestured at the gathered group. "The way I see it, you already have two strong ones here. *This* one actually owes me his life," Mornik pointed to Cruso. "I use divine fire, but much of my group already knows at least one ranged spell."

Yedrak jerked a thumb toward Urgosk, "But I want to keep an eye on this one. He stinks of trouble."

Mornik looked beyond Yedrak, only to see Urgosk throw an amused smirk at the warrior-priest's back. As a matter of racial pride, the dwarves weren't fond of working with orcs when they were going to fight orcs, but he decided to hold off judgment. Mornik only replied, "I've learned that trouble often comes from the direction you aren't looking."

"Show me your group," Yedrak bade.

Only moments later, Mornik returned alone, holding the blue tile bearing eighteen. The dwarf asked, "Sir Cruso, would you kindly introduce me to the rest of our group?"

Cruso made all the introductions as requested. When done, Mornik looked over the knight and commented. "Someone seems to have done a fine job finishing your healing. You weren't infected, I trust?"

Vallese and Allisee took a step back when Mornik mentioned 'infected.' Allisee inquired, "Does this have something to do with your wounds at the monastery?"

Cruso nodded, "Mornik and I met when he helped me out of a bind."

Allisee turned her head to speak to Mornik, though her eyes stayed on Cruso as she spoke, "Tell us more."

The dwarf hopped onto a small barrel as he gave his story. "Kashmer has quite a large district set aside for those of us who aren't giants." The dwarf stood four feet, ten inches tall. Even with the barrel helping, it only brought his eyes level to the tops of their heads. "Exploration is in my blood, and I set out for a walk. I happened across one of the ramps leading down to the waste tunnels beneath the city.

Those tunnels produce the worst odor, as you can imagine. The access gate at the bottom was left open. Curiously enough, the workers had left their tools sitting outside, unguarded."

Mornik patted his hammer, Heel. "Kashmer's tunnel workers are usually dwarves or gnomes, and we care a lot about our tools and crafts. Odd they would lie abandoned outside. I thought to venture closer. When I did, I heard the unmistakable sounds of combat. Grunting, swearing, a war cry as steel hit something solid. I beseeched Nandorrin for support, then…"

"Nandorrin?" Vallese asked.

Mornik gestured to his tabard, which covered the layers of a scale mail coat. The tabard displayed a forge in red and gold colors. The group noticed a similar coloring on his shield. Interwoven red and gold plates of metal simulated a burning fire. "Nandorrin is God of Fire and the Forge. He is Grand-Master-Smith. He is Keeper of the Forge Flame."

Urgosk interrupted, "Does he cook too?"

The dwarf stared hard at the orc's smirk. "Nay, but he'll provide the fire and expect dullards to be smart enough not to get *burnt*."

Vallese's face pinched in confusion. "I thought…you barred your gods? How can they help you?"

Mornik didn't seem to mind the interruption of his story. He began lecturing as a wise man might. "The gods barred themselves out of Dhea Loral after the folly of the Godswars nearly destroyed everything. However, they still can affect the world through their followers. As a disciple of Nandorrin, I serve his interests in the world, channeling his divine power through my humble form. As I expect you'll see in the coming battle, I can both cause and remedy a great many wounds in his name."

Swinging his eyes to the rest of the group, he continued.

"Now, as I was recalling, I could tell a battle brewed under the streets. I rushed into the smelly filth of the city. The workers carry their own magical or divine lights, and those lit the tunnel ahead. More importantly, the lights illuminated their bodies. Three of them were laid low by claw and bite marks."

Mornik made a quick motion on behalf of the dead, touching two fingers to his lips and pointing them skyward. "The last lie at an intersection, where I daresay another rescuer stood." Mornik gestured to Sir Cruso. "Dressed then as he is now, you can imagine he looked out of place in the waste tunnels. He was too busy to notice me. He wielded sword against a pair of mariner ghouls." He noticed Vallese flinch and her eyebrows scrunch inward questioningly. Rather than be interrupted, he described them. "Err…men who died at sea to other unliving, and now have become ghouls themselves. Their lungs are always filled with water, gurgling as they approach. The touch of their claws drains the strength of muscles from the living. They stay in wet places. They must have found a way up from the harbor."

Noting that Vallese looked horrified at the description, Mornik returned to the point of the story. "I arrived just in time. They overwhelmed this brave man. I could see his muscles weakening. The sword slipped from his grasp. The ghouls would have made him their next meal."

Sir Cruso shifted uncomfortably, and Mornik gave him a reassuring pat on the back. "You did a brave thing; you just lacked the proper tools. I didn't even have to use Brozek…excuse me. *Heel* in your Hespal tongue," he glanced at Cruso as he hefted his sizeable hammer. "All the better anyway, a touch from them could have made me another victim. I revealed to them Nandorrin's blessed flame. The unliving are burned by the sight of the Holy Flame. Even wet ones catch fire! A Holy Flame and some divine chanting, and they were charred to the bone."

The dwarf priest laid a hand on the Cruso's arm. "Alas, I saved this knight, but the workers didn't survive. I performed the rites to make sure they would not one day rise as unliving. I lack the same proficiency in healing diseases, and I suggested to the young human that he seek a priest who could properly treat those wounds."

"You are adept enough! Most of my wounds disappeared like magic!" Cruso testified.

"Divinity," Mornik clarified, "not magic."

Allisee interrupted, glancing between Mornik and Cruso. "Others might have run to grab a guard instead."

Sir Cruso straightened, "I have trained my whole life for fighting. It isn't in my nature to run."

Mornik looked at him directly, "Which is why I'm sticking close to you when we go into this war against hills full of orcs. You owe me your life; I expect you to be there for me."

"Just one thing," Cruso turned to face the elf. "We have now been entreated with the tale of my injuries. I have yet to hear the tale of yours."

Allisee stared evenly into his eyes. "Some tales aren't so easily shared."

Volume 1, Chapter 3   **"Sailing South"**

Privateers shared cramped quarters underneath the top deck as *Lancer* sailed alongside other Kashmer galleons similarly packed with adventurers. Folk grumbled and let off tempers. Kashmer's marines were forced to intercede at the first sign of raised voices. Oddly enough, this helped some new groups to band together quicker than they normally would. Prior to the voyage, the navy created separate group sleeping areas with partition sheets, made of the cheapest, most readily-available sources. Many of these had holes and unappetizing smells. Once the privateers took up residence, the area became further segregated as new blankets, coats, and other makeshift linens were hung. The deck became a honeycombed maze and, as more than one privateer commented, a potentially disastrous fire trap. Illumination was restricted to magical or divine sources, and several spell casters made quick money selling lightstones.

Only a few groups at a time were allowed to venture up to the open deck above, so as not to get in the way of the working sailors. This meant most parties stayed holed up in their group's honeycomb cell, forced to spend time with their new companions. A few lucky groups had access to an open port window, allowing for some fresh, salty air to carry away the stink. They received the most visitors; as many sought simply a view of the outside. Unfortunately, the occasional green-faced conscripts would run to those openings to eject their last meal. From the port side of the ship, they could make out the shoreline of their home continent, Quoros. In the evening, they saw the lights of the village of Estlof, but the ships didn't stop.

Allisee voiced her displeasure at sharing such cramped quarters with the men. Encouraging Vallese to do likewise, they struck a deal with the occupants in the next cell. That night, all the men from both groups shared one space, the women shared the other side of a thick blanket wall. This left the men to deal with the full auditory assault of Mornik's rumbling snores. By morning, the women returned and the other men went back to their group.

During the morning hours, a visitor slipped into their bunk area. All five members of group eighteen were keeping to themselves, making their own private preparations for the upcoming battle. They looked up so see a young, short, woman greeting them with a smile. She carried a lute case upon her back, but a different musical instrument in her hand. Dark hair fell about her shoulders. Her style of dress seemed to favor the southern city of Orlaun, ruffles at the collars and sleeves, yet she revealed more skin than fashionable in that city. A mole on her right cheek was the only interruption of her smooth skin. She displayed four rings of various stones and designs upon her fingers, two necklaces (one of which supported a glowing lightstone), and a mix of gem studs and hoops between both ears.

"Greetings! I don't believe I've had the pleasure yet. Do any of you know me?"

Sir Cruso set aside the small journal he often read. "Merissa Delroy! I have seen you perform in Chime Plaza!"

The woman blushed as she dipped into a curtsey. "Aye! And hopefully you enjoyed the performance."

"Of course!"

"Chime Plaza? Is that in Kashmer?" Allisee asked.

Sir Cruso noted that the same question seemed to hang in everyone else's eyes. He faced the others and explained. "Chime Plaza is an open park. It sits at the three-way junction of Salvation Street, the Harbor District, and the Merchant District. Musicians and artists of all kinds can be found aplenty there. They have performances on midweek day."

Mornik sat up in his hammock, releasing a loud grunt as he did. "Just music? Any storytellers? Historians?"

Merissa flashed him a smile, "You can find recitations of history there. We have many chroniclers willing to share the old fables. I see we have a couple of you who share indulgences in exploring culture?"

Urgosk snapped his fingers, drawing everyone's attention. "I think we're missing the big question…what is *that*?" His pointing finger indicated the strange instrument in her hands. The cylindrical device was thicker on the top end where she held the handle, but tapered down to a point on the floor. Strings stretched from end to end on every facing of the instrument. A stringed bow in Merissa's other hand seemed to accompany it.

"This is an oblian. Heard of it?" As each shook their heads, Merissa held the instrument upright, resting on the floor. "The bow creates the music, though you need to spin it at times to reach all the notes."

She demonstrated, drawing the bowstring across the oblian's taut strings. Even as the bow moved back and forth, her other hand would spin the instrument one way and then the next to reach the desired strings. "Or, you can play it this way." With a deft swing, the bottom point of the instrument swung up and came to rest on her left shoulder. She continued to play notes on it very similar in style to a violin, while spinning the oblian's pointed base on a worn leather patch sewn onto her shoulder.

The others allowed themselves to be entranced by the music, though after the first chorus Vallese asked, "Where did you find that?" Even as the dusk-skinned woman asked, she held her unstrung bowstaff closer to the oblian. She seemed to be comparing her weapon against the instrument.

Merissa set the oblian's point upon the floor. "The Republic of Pluetlo. It's a cultural symbol there, very popular." Vallese's face fell slightly at the news, so the musician asked, "Why do you ask?"

Vallese indicated the weapon in her hands. "I thought to compare the wood to that of my bowstaff. I am Vallese…" A slight pause, then added "Foxblood."

Cruso noted the pause. When they first met he had asked her about a surname, she had no answer. The knight wasn't sure whether it was reluctance or confusion over the meaning.

Vallese asked Merissa, "Have you traveled a lot?"

"Aye. I've lived my life traveling with different troupes, entertaining caravans and sailors as we journeyed."

Vallese offered the bow. "Have you ever seen wood like this?"

Merissa examined it. Turning it over in her hands and caressing its length. "A dark wood. Compact growth rings. Good sturdiness and flexibility, proper for a bow." She handed it back graciously. "I can't say that I have, but I'm no expert in wood nor trees. Where does it come from?"

"My homeland."

Examining the other woman from head to toe, Merissa couldn't be sure of her ethnicity. "Where is your homeland?"

Vallese took some time to answer. She finally admitted, "I don't know."

Merissa looked at Vallese with compassionate eyes. "I bet there is a tale to that." The musician watched as Vallese's eyes widened in fright, and the woman shrunk back into her bedroll. Merissa decided not to pursue her questions. Instead, her eyes glided over each of the five groupmates.

She decided it was time to get to the point of her visit. "I've been visiting all the groups, chatting with them. A few of them have become well-acquainted with their new friends; others seem a little more withdrawn. So, tell me, have you come up with a plan if we land on a beach full of mad orcs?"

Urgosk grabbed a flask hanging from his neck. He raised it in a mock toast as he declared, "We fight and clear a path of blood! We trod over our dead enemies! I am of the First Hand, a member of the bravest warriors in my tribe! I stand for them."

Sir Cruso reached to the side while Urgosk spoke. As the half-orc reached the crest of his proclamation, the knight raised his shield and added, "I will lead with my shield and protect those behind me. I am a protector and warrior. My shield is for others, as much as for me."

Merissa held up a hand, stalling Mornik even as the dwarf opened his mouth to join them. "I don't want to hear your tiles speaking. I want to hear about you."

This silenced the others, and they thought on her meaning. The minstrel continued, "The Kashmer Navy decided on the tile method to try to evenly balance teams of privateers. This was a refined concept of something Katressa Bilil did when she organized teams of privateers to fight in the Stonelands. It sounds like a great concept for balance…the god Foyul would likely be pleased. However, we know we are much more than our tiles say. It is better to know our companions for their specific qualities than the general ones the navy assigned. Did any of you feel you could have grabbed a different tile?"

Most remained silent, but Urgosk spoke up. "I, Urgosk, could have picked from the warrior tiles as easily as from the scout. I'm a good scout and sneaker, but when a fight starts, I cut through anything in my way. It just seemed that there were too many red tiles and not enough black."

During his response, the others of the group heeded Merissa's meaning and took a deeper look at Urgosk. The half-orc looked as sturdy and heavy as either Sir Cruso or the dwarf, but he stood at only 5'7". His brownish-gray skin stretched taut over a muscular frame. His face displayed a flattened nose. Two underbite tusks stood out from his lips. The others had already noted his habit of picking his teeth with long, jagged, broken nails, before wiping the resulting sludge on whatever furniture proved handy. His teeth were yellow with some brown, and his eyes featured red irises staring out from yellow orbs. The sides and back of his head were shaved close. This left long, greasy, black strands of hair growing from only the top of his head, extending down to both shoulders. Two earrings sparkled from his left ear, but his torn right ear bore testimony of the painful separation of whatever earrings once adorned it.

"Is there a story behind that weapon?" The minstrel asked, pointing to the dwarf-crafted warhammer hanging from Urgosk's belt.

Mornik sat forward on his hammock, obviously interested in such a tale. When Urgosk looked down at the weapon, his face betrayed amusement.

"This? Ha-ra, ha-ra!" He drew it and ran his fingers along the back-spike protruding opposite the hammerhead. Although the design bore similarities to Heel, this was a small weapon made for one hand. "Nay, this is my door-opener!"

Mornik sputtered, "A…a what? You use that like a crowbar?!?!"

Urgosk shrugged even as Mornik looked indignant, "Whenever I don't just use my axe to open the door, or split the chest. This spike and handle offers excellent grip. I've breached a few barricades with it, wrenched a few lids."

Mornik demanded, "And where did you get that?"

"Battlefield trophy."

The dwarf's eyes began to turn fierce, but Urgosk added, "From looting other orcs."

Merissa decided to steer the conversation away from subjects which could harm the party's relationships. "Urgosk, what is your main weapon?"

Urgosk reached behind his seat. He pulled forth a huge, two-headed axe. The top ends of both blades stuck upward like spikes. Leather cords wrapped about the handle. Colorful rocks ornamented the leather wrap.

"This is my battle-mate. Clears any enemies in my way."

Cruso pointed to Urgosk's armor and said, "If given the opportunity, we could have done something about those links back in Kashmer."

Urgosk's chain shirt, his only real protection from blows, extended to mid-thigh. Cloth underpadding kept it from pinching his skin. Even those not very familiar with armor noted the visible patchwork repairs on the worn item. Cruso's observation seemed centered on the tears along the arm openings and the neckline. The shirt's original design was present in places, where links tightened around a definitive edge. However, bent and broken links bordered the edges of the neck and sleeves in places, widening the original openings.

Urgosk glanced at them, "Oh, I did that."

Cruso's jaw dropped as Mornik "hmphed" and shook his head. The dwarf dropped back into his hammock. The half-orc flexed his arms as he explained. "Too tight. Needed more freedom."

Merissa cleared her throat, turning her head to Sir Cruso. "And how about you; are you more than a red tile? Your shield, for example, a family crest?"

The shield held in Cruso's hand bore a figure, the head and neck of a white horse. The image rested on a background pattern of alternating green and yellow diamonds.

"As I spoke, my shield is for others as much as for me. Sir Cruso Lanvyrl, at everyone's service." He paused to stand and give a formal bow, before returning to his seat. "This is the Lanvyrl family crest."

Merissa pegged his appearance, mannerisms, and accent perfectly, "What interest do the Counties of Diara have in this?"

She didn't miss his barely perceptible flinch. "Nay interest. I'm here on my own."

Allisee looked as if she planned to voice a question, but Mornik asked the one on her mind. "Are you lord of an estate?"

Cruso shook his head, but hesitated before answering. Merissa guessed that he didn't have a simple answer to that question. He spoke, "I do not have a title that grants me land or property. I'm traveling and finding my own place in the world."

Merissa knew that generally a knight held fealty to someone. She took a second appraisal of him, confirming that he did indeed seem the part. Cruso's brown eyes stared out from under thick, brown eyebrows. His mustache and beard were neatly trimmed in a style fitting for the genteel folk of Diara. Merissa couldn't help but notice that he was the tallest member of the group, if not one of the tallest men on the ship. His arms and shoulders were thick…likely an even match for the strong half-orc.

The navy vessel had no shortage of wardrobe dummies in order to properly hang armor. Sir Cruso's polished armor adorned one such dummy, except for one item. Cruso wore his chain shirt. The care that went into his armor put Urgosk's torn chain to shame. The armor displayed on the stand included a multitude of pieces Merissa had witnessed covering almost every inch of a jousting knight's body. Both a breastplate and pauldrons bore decorations of horses etched into the steel. Metal gauntlets encasing leather gloves joined with forearm bracers. Thigh and shin guards were bridged with poleyns. None of it appeared easy to don without help. A helm decorated with a plume of white horse hair topped the display. Few warriors on board carried armor of such extent. It spoke of wealth and influence, whereas the owner's appearance did not. Cruso's once-fine clothes were marked with stains of both dirt and blood specks. The seam at his right shoulder had started to come loose and his shirt displayed a tear near one of the blood spots.

She waved at the armor set. "Do you have a squire to assist you?"

"I anticipate Brother Heavyboot to be of assistance in that regard."

"Wait…what?" The dwarf sat up, swinging his legs over the edge of his hammock. "How do you 'anticipate' such a thing?"

Sir Cruso smiled, "As I recall, you requested the honor of myself as your guardian in this land of savages. I'll need to be properly outfitted to play my role. More armor means less demand on your healing talents. As long as I'm standing strong, nay foes will lay hands on the healer."

Mornik stared at the armor quietly for a few heartbeats. "Fine, fine. And you're going to stand up on your promise? You'll keep up a brave fight nay matter what?"

Sir Cruso straightened, "Honor is everything, Valor a close second."

Mornik nodded, relaxing back into the hammock. "I'll help you, but you better have your own method of taking a piss wearing that."

"Easy. There is a latch there…"

As his hand indicated the codpiece of the outfit, Merissa decided once again to alter the course of conversation. "Two swords? Why?"

"This silver-layered one is a family heirloom. It represents the Lanvyrl family heir. I use a baldric to hold this one on my back." Sir Cruso let Merissa examine it as he drew forth a second sword made of steel. "This one I helped forge. It feels more familiar to me. Plus, this steel is built for proper combat. The silver one is for monsters vulnerable to such alloys. Shapechangers and such. The silver blade needs more care."

"Similar reason behind that dagger as well? I believe it looks like plain iron?" she asked.

The others could see a dagger and sheath strapped to the steel sword's scabbard. As the minstrel observed, it had a rough iron look to it.

"Aye," he confirmed, "Some monsters recoil from such iron. One must be prepared for anything. I also carry a parrying dagger." The others could see it hanging from the back of Cruso's belt. "And a folded crossbow."

Merissa had wondered about the metal-and-wood bundle resting near Cruso's spot. Now that he explained it, she could see how the spring arms were folded back over the stock. Next to it sat the small journal Cruso had set down when she peeked into their cell. It drew her attention.

"Did I interrupt a good book?"

"An important one, but I know all the words. I still find solace reading it." He handed it to her. Merissa turned a few pages, recognizing several quotes and stanzas. Cruso explained even as she read. "A collection of important words and wisdom from *The Codex*. It is my spiritual guide."

Merissa snuck a sly glance at the others as he mentioned the religious document. Most showed little reaction at all. The half-orc rolled his eyes. The elf held such a neutral face, that it almost seemed forced. Merissa handed the journal back and decided to focus on someone new.

Although the elf was one of the quietest members, the minstrel noticed she seemed to be the subtlest observer. If anyone on the ship could cause Merissa to be jealous, it would be Allisee's grace and beauty. Long, blonde hair spilled to mid-back, though a decorative hairpiece held some of it up in a knot. The hair fell just below breasts that were humble enough, yet complimented the elf's perfect, lithe build. Merissa had noticed that Allisee seemed to glide wherever she roamed, despite the rocking waves and narrow passages. Her clothing of blue and purple dyes were more often reserved for nobility. The finest silk, imported from the far away Republic of Lar, hugged her figure as only a fine tailor could customize. Allisee's outfits reflected opulence, not battle.

"You do not look as if you are walking into battle. I may have heard your name in passing, but we haven't been introduced."

"I am Allisee Lentara. I am nay warrior. Although I have been trained in this..." She indicated a scabbard on her bed which seemed to house a long, thin blade. "I rely more on spells."

"Are you a wizard, sorceress, or something else entirely?"

"What's the difference?" Interrupted Urgosk. "Magic is magic, whether they study it or the gods grant it."

Mornik once again sat up with a huff. "Hold that thought, blasphemer! We priests don't use magic. We channel miracles from our gods! Our source is divinity, not some witchcraft or street tricks."

"Excuse us; but we are having a conversation now." Allisee gently reprimanded her companions. As Mornik resettled into his hammock and Urgosk took a sip from his flask, the elf returned her attention to the minstrel. "I'm a sorceress. My spells came to me rather introspectively."

"Ah, a sorceress. So your magic isn't taught or learned, its part of your bloodline." Merissa replied, though her explanation seemed aimed at the others.

"Beg pardon," said Sir Cruso. Both women noted that at least one of Allisee's companions practiced manners. "But what does that mean, exactly?"

Merissa spoke when Allisee didn't immediately reply. "It means that some natural magic runs in her family. Perhaps through a spell, curse, unnatural union, or providence, magic passes along her family tree. It's not something that another can teach; you learn through self-discovery. Do you know how magic entered your family line?"

"Nay."

By Allisee's curt response, Merissa was versed enough to know a lie when she heard one. Deciding to avoid any confrontations again, she asked, "What spells can you offer your companions in battle? I see a wand on your belt."

The elf patted the wand. "This enacts a barrier for my own protection, for a brief time. My spells manifest in the wind and in lightning. I can draw fog around us for cover. My touch can channel lightning into an opponent or cast it afar."

Allisee appeared not to notice, but as she described her abilities, Vallese edged away from the elf. Vallese also wrapped her arms about herself, fending off a chill Merissa could not feel.

Mornik chuckled, "Hmm, seems I don't need to help you with your armor after all, Sir. I'll just follow the woman throwing lightning around the field."

Allisee looked at him. "The effort drains me. If we're going into a large battle, I'll need to conserve my energy."

"It's good for all of you to know the strengths and limitations of your companions. And your staff?" The minstrel pointed to the four-foot, decorative walking stick at Allisee's side.

"Well, it can store some of my spell energy for me, but not a great amount. This is a simple traveler's staff; its best use is thus." Wielding the staff, she cupped one hand and tipped the upper end of the staff into that hand. A conjured food delight appeared. Allisee offered it to Merissa. "Care for a nut-cake?"

Merissa accepted it with a gracious laugh. "I see. A traveler's staff offers nourishment for the road."

"I'll have one," Urgosk barked.

"Sorry, once a day only. It can also shrink down in size at command. I could leave it in my pack if I have nay need of it."

Mornik asked, "Think I've seen one before. Do you hail from Thellistae?"

"I do." Allisee kept her smile, but Merissa could once again sense a guarded tone in her voice.

"Ooh!" The dwarf cracked a smile, "I could ask you many questions about the ruins and dragonlore."

"And not one could I answer," Allisee was quick to reply. "It is forbidden."

Merissa quickly shifted focus. "And you, Heavyboot? Where is home?"

"I hail from Paradise," Mornik's toothy smile emerged from the depths of his brownish-red beard.

He seemed content to let the comment hang there for anyone to attempt a jest. Merissa, however, was well-traveled enough to pick up on his meaning. "In Southern Quoros? Kingdom of Gheras?"

"The very same, although a little north of it. A quick stroll up and across the nearby river ferry. My clan digs deep into the mountains, carving out the finest gems you will ever lay eyes upon."

She looked over his stocky frame. If standing upright, he would still stand shy of five feet. The dwarf carried a shield that matched the height of Sir Cruso's, but might look absurdly big in the hands of the shorter dwarf. Like Cruso's, it bore decoration. Unlike Cruso's, the overlapping red and gold plates that covered it, symbolizing fire, did not appear to be a family crest.

"And I believe we've established that you are their priest? Tell me more," She prodded.

"With pleasure!" Mornik enthusiastically hopped out of his hammock. His namesake heavy boots thundered up a puff of dust as he rattled a floorboard. Thick fingers fished a length of chain out from under his beard, delivering his holy symbol into their sight. The iron adornment featured twin hammers crossed over a forge, matching the red-and-gold design on his tabard. "Nandorrin, God of Fire and the Forge. I'm on a pilgrimage in his good name. If you'll allow me a moment, minstrel, I'll tell my own story. I'm up to your tricks."

Merissa's eyes widened a fraction, but enough for the others to notice.

Heavyboot continued, "Getting the small-clan to learn of ourselves before the battle? You're having us open up and discover more about ourselves. Well, I'll do my own explanations without help, thank you."

The minstrel threw her hands up in mock surrender, while the others looked upon Mornik with new appraisal. The priest passed his glance over them in return.

"Put your ear to the ground. There, you will hear the heartbeat of Epos Goth. It is a heartbeat kept in rhythm by the steady blows of pickaxes and hammers of my people. We live on the surface, but we thrive in the Deeprealm. Before the Godswars, the Underways allowed us to trade great distances under your shallow seas and rivers. When the gods tore the continents, the Underways were fractured. Alas, much has been lost. Maybe some of it can be rediscovered. My search has been delayed by Kashmer's need of my services…so be it. I may support you in several ways."

He reached over to grab his hammer. Large as it was, it looked as if he could use it easily enough with one hand if he chose. Rows of small teeth adorned the hammer's front, trailed by a spike sticking to the rear. "As you've already heard, this is Heel, called 'Brozek' in my tongue. Nandorrin's blessings, offered by my Uncle Vermact, lend it the strength of the faithful."

Mornik turned his free hand upward. Hissing a command, fire sprung from his palm without searing his flesh. The group watched the fire dance in his hand as he continued. "Nandorrin grants me dominion over the element of fire. I can reshape it, summon it, throw it, or use smoke to cloud us from our enemies. As you already know," Mornik paused to glance at Cruso, "I can draw from his divinity to heal your wounds." The dwarf reached over and hefted a shoulder bag. "The bottles in here are healing potions. A last resort in case my efforts drain my strength. Although, if you need to get these yourself, I'd appreciate you pouring one in my mouth to get me back up."

Mornik set aside his equipment and resumed his seat in the hammock. Breaking the sudden silence, Merissa asked, "Brew those yourself?"

"Nay. I hope to master that craft someday soon."

Now that the priest had perceptively revealed Merissa's game, all eyes shifted to the one companion who hadn't been questioned. Vallese shrunk from the attention. Her face and body turned away, though her eyes attempted a subtle scan from face to face. The group studied her in return, looking to decipher any clues about the woman.

Her darker skin tone was uncommon in Kashmer. Dark hair fell about her shoulders, revealing hints of red when bright light played across it. The odd, impractical armor she wore tended to highlight her body's assets. Her athletic frame supported more inches on her bust and hips than Allisee. A pattern of tattooed spots flowed around her shoulders and lower legs. The other blemish upon her skin could be found in the form of numerous scars on her arms, partly covered by cloth wraps. If Merissa had to guess her age, she would say Vallese was still in the prime of her youth.

Merissa felt that she had to approach her questions carefully. "Is that bow your primary weapon?"

"Aye."

When nothing more was said, the minstrel indicated the length of wood leaning near the woman. "And that staff?" Unlike the bow's strange wood, Merissa could tell the staff was crafted from rosewood. It had a leather cord running partway along its length, perhaps to sling it over one's shoulder?

Vallese pulled the staff closer. "I crafted it. Carved it." Her fingers traced the leaf designs running patterns around the shaft.

Urgosk snorted, "This will take all day! Relax, open up more. You already know about us. You say you don't remember your homeland?"

Vallese's eyes widened at the half-orc. Merissa wanted to scold him for his blunt nature. The dark-skinned woman struggled to continue. "I remember…small…"

"Little?" Urgosk offered.

Vallese's eyes began to narrow again, this time dangerously, at the half-orc. She continued in her strange accent. "Hespal is not my birth tongue. I still learn it."

Urgosk held out an open palm, "Well, that's something about you! What is your language?"

The rosewood staff swung about so quickly that it was pointed an inch away from Urgosk's throat before the others even flinched. She stared him down before uttering a stream of words none of them could interpret. Her tongue clicked on her teeth several times. The foreign language was unlike any they had heard before. The only clues to her meaning were the daggers in her stare.

When finished, she set the staff down and looked away from him. "That is my tongue. If you know it, you can tell me what it is."

Merissa opened her mouth to speak, but Vallese raised a hand in warning. "I am not good with questions. I will say what I will say, like Mornik." She took a deep breath. Another slight pause to think through her words, during which time Merissa and Allisee threw scolding looks at Urgosk. "I was young when taken from home. Some day I will find my way back. I do remember things."

She pointed a finger at her scanty armor. "This armor of which you jest, it is more than our warriors wore. It serves me. My bow and my staff will serve you. I'm good with them. I don't like magic." Her statement caused Allisee's head to turn. Vallese tilted her head up proudly, daring the elf to argue anything. "If I face magic-user on battlefield, they die first. I nay let magic get me unprepared again. If we need food or supplies in the wilds, I can find them. I know secrets of animals. I ask and they share their spirit." Vallese ran a hand over the pouches and pockets on her hip. The group couldn't know of the odd collection of animal trophies they contained. An owl feather, tuft of panther hair, bear claw, and fox tail among them.

The others puzzled over what that meant as she continued. "We go into this as tribe. Or…what Mornik said…small-clan. My fortune and fate are tied with yours. I stand with you."

When she went silent, no one dared to be the first to speak. Finally, Cruso leaned forward. "If I may. Yesterday you had no surname, today…Foxblood?"

Her eyes wandered somewhere distant. "It is what they called me once." And she said no more on the subject.

When the fleet turned toward the shoreline, and the time had come for the landing, tensions ran high. The drawn-out nature of the landing made everything worse. *Lancer* aligned with other vessels in a long line. A leadsman sounded off the depth of the water as the ship sailed, while crew readied smaller skiffs to take the invasion force to the beach. Those privateers less knowledgeable had asked why the ships didn't go all the way to the shore, while others sniggered at their naivete. A few seemed ready to wet their leggings at the thought of rowing the smaller boats to shore under a hail of orc arrows.

First Mate Vanford even paused in his duties to curse at some of the mumblers. "*Lancer* will protect your landing using our rock slings and ballistae. The orcs didn't know we were landing here until just now. You won't find an organized fight at the beach."

Kashmer's fleet picked a spot where the sandy shoreline spanned between ten and twenty meters wide. Beyond that lay a mix of small woods, rocky outcroppings, and distant hills. Group eighteen waited their turn as the first wave rowed for the beach. Cruso, Urgosk, Mornik, Vallese, and Allisee struggled for a good viewpoint as they watched the skiffs cross the shallows. Arrows flew from behind the trees and rocks on the shore. Mariners and privateers alike cried out in agony as some arrows found their mark among the boats. The fleet responded swiftly with all ships firing nearly in unison. Despite having a hard time seeing individual targets, slings and bolts arced out and sprayed across the land.

A few spells launched from the skiffs. Cruso and Urgosk elbowed each other for a better vantage when a score of firework-like bursts illuminated a distant ridge.

"Only an illusion," Allisee noted, and the eyes of the group turned to her. "It may seem real if you're caught in it, but that was merely a well-crafted illusion."

A melody rolled across the waves from *Lancer*. Merissa stood at the front of the ship, oblian resting on one shoulder as she played it like a fiddle, her lute slung over her back. She played a stirring ballad known to many. The subject involved a scene from a popular play, in which a warrior girded himself for battle after an insult to his lady. The hastening tempo of notes gave encouragement to those heading into battle.

The group could do nothing until the boats returned to ferry them across. They watched helplessly but with great interest as the first skiffs touched the shore. The distant sounds of war cries could be heard.

Kashmer's fleet let loose its final barrage then went still. They could no longer fire without a chance of stones raining on their forces. The soldiers and privateers waiting on the ships watched as more eye-catching spells went off along the shore. Magical bolts and scorching streams of fire flourished up and down the beach. Instead of a line of soldiers, the individual privateer groups charged across the sand as soon as their skiffs allowed. Some of the privateers on the beach twisted or fell as distant arrows struck. Group eighteen couldn't see much of the fighting. It didn't sound like there were many orcs on the shore, but they couldn't really see anything from the ship.

Urgosk seemed to barely contain his energy. He shifted from foot to foot, changing his grip on his battleaxe frequently. Cruso glanced at his companion and noticed something…or at least, the lack of something.

"I thought you said you were going to wear war-paint?"

The half-orc turned his tusky grin toward the taller human. "I am. But war-paint is best taken from my enemies."

It took the knight a moment to figure it out. "You smear their blood on your face?"

Urgosk nodded, even as Mornik and Vallese unconsciously stepped away from him. "Spoils of conquest make the best war-paint. Especially blood."

The others turned their attention back to the distant fighting. Vanford's prediction about the lack of an organized defense by the orcs appeared to be accurate. Kashmer forces swarmed up the beach and into cover with few casualties. There may have been only orc scouts on the shore, though it felt as if eyes were behind every rock. The boats returned, allowing group eighteen their chance to join the landing forces. Allisee and Vallese descended the rope ladder gracefully.

As Cruso put hands on the ladder, Mornik spoke. "After the time and effort I spent helping you buckle on all that metal, you better not slip and fall into that water."

"I am touched by your concern, good priest, but fear not. I am less burdened than I might appear." Sir Cruso replied as he swung his legs over the edge.

He wore the full suit of armor. Shield strapped to his back along with the silver sword, steel sword at his side, folded crossbow on his opposite hip; half the group feared they would be watching him drop and drown. The knight climbed down with ease, showing no impairment from his metal shell. Cruso took hold of one of the spare oars.

Mornik proved to have more trouble. The dwarf priest cursed in his native tongue as the rope ladder shook. Similar to the knight, Mornik had numerous items strapped to his body, but he failed to carry his weight as well as Cruso

"Watch yer own descent, Heavyboot!" Urgosk called from above. "Ha-ra, ha-ra!"

Both Allisee and Vallese gripped the sides of the boat with concern. Cruso and one of the rowers helped Mornik down the last couple steps. In comparison, Urgosk practically ran down the climbing ladder with ease. Only at the last rung did he falter and cry out, "Ah, help!" The boat rocked as everyone reacted at once, moving toward or away from him. But his exclamation proved a ruse, and he lithely dropped to a seat and grabbed an oar. He openly chuckled as the rest resumed their seats and the boat settled.

Vallese admonished, "This not play time!"

Urgosk, between chuckles, replied. "We live, we endure hard times and fear, then we die. Somewhere in that existence ya have to make time to laugh, or what good is life?"

Mornik, glaring at Urgosk, commented. "Hard to believe someone can be so wise yet so stupid at the same time."

The boat had room to cram two groups, so they waited as a second group descended from the ship.

*

Rowing for the beach at a frantic pace, Urgosk turned his head to Sir Cruso and spoke, "This plan has all the makin's of a nightmare. Ya agree?" When the knight only responded with a noncommittal shrug, the half-orc pressed for more. "Do high-bred Diarans 'ave nightmares? Anything disrupt yer opulent dreams?"

Sir Cruso's eyes kept busy scanning the approaching beach. Each stroke brought them closer to war cries and the hissing of spells. Much of the action remained obscured by the treeline and first small hills.

The knight responded to Urgosk's question. "It may seem tame to you, but I do have dreadful dreams centered around an opulent house. That's all I will say on the subject. How about yourself? Do orcs have nightmares?"

Urgosk chuckled, "Aye, we 'ave nightmares. But even in my worst dreams, all my friends are dancin' and drinkin'."

Their boat slid into the sandy beach without incident. They could hear yelling and screaming beyond the trees. They managed to disembark before the group accompanying them. Allisee, keenly aware of her spell-casting appearance and likelihood as a target, hurried them. "We'll find no protection standing on this sand. We need to move forward and find a better position. Hopefully before others claim it!"

"I see a game trail leading into the rocks, there!" Vallese pointed and started forward.

The rest began running at a jog. From the side came a mounted horsewoman, dressed in a Kashmer Navy officer uniform. She shouted commands to the privateers and mariners. "You may fight as your separate groups, but stay in a unified line! We will move as a wave up the hill! Don't stray out of sight!"

Sir Cruso shook his head, "They expect an untrained rabble to move separately while staying in a line? This will be chaos!"

As she galloped past, Mornik spoke, "How did she get a horse over here so fast?"

"Magic," replied the elf.

The dwarf huffed, "I sought more than the obvious answer!"

As they raced to the rocks, Sir Cruso and Urgosk stretched their legs into the lead positions. Both warriors crested the first ridge without incident. They were outlined against the backdrop of the fleet, but no arrows sought them out. The land before them formed a series of ridges, capped by brush. Their eyes swept across everything. Neither saw any orcs, but there were countless hiding places for an archer. They could hear and see groups of privateers and mariners scattered ahead and to both sides. Despite the words of the officer on horseback, there seemed to be little order among their forces. Some groups held back as the ships continued to empty, others pressed forward, eager to meet the enemy. The tunes of Merissa's instrument still carried across the water, inspiring those who could hear them.

The half-orc gave the knight an unexpected slap on the back. "Ya run good carrying that metal can."

"Thanks for the compli…"

"But not fast enough to steal the first kill from me."

The knight stared. "Did you just offer challenge?"

Urgosk smiled, lips revealing more of his lower tusks. "It is like…how do they say? The gauntlet is thrown."

Sir Cruso's gaze was hard, but a slow smile formed. "So, you do speak like a Diaran! Very well, sir, challenge accepted."

Allisee and Vallese came atop the ridge. The elf pointed to the trailing dwarf. "You'd best remember the speed at which your healer can run. We can move at an easy pace until action pushes us to call upon our strength."

Urgosk turned back with upraised eyebrows. "That *was* an easy pace!"

"If I can't see you," Vallese spoke curtly, "I can't help you."

Mornik huffed in breaths as he paused alongside his companions. He waved his hands apart, clearly trying to buy a moment to catch his breath before speaking. Sir Cruso scanned ahead and voiced his opinion first. "We can't stay exposed up here. We should keep moving."

"And I've a challenge to win!" Said the half-orc as he propelled himself forward.

In an attempt to regain some order, Allisee took charge. As they advanced, she called out directions to the two warriors. She fed their eagerness, calling out potential ambush spots and sending one or the other to investigate. Sir Cruso and Urgosk played along, moving sideways as much as forward, checking blind spots, but overall allowing for Mornik to keep pace easier.

"Would 'ave my first kill already if not for all yer noise." Urgosk called.

Sir Cruso kept up banter as well, "They're running from my armor!"

Allisee grew concerned as she looked about. Kashmer's forces could be seen spreading over a wide area. Many hills placed the ships out of sight. Fighting could be heard, though it came sporadically. Her senses focused everywhere. The heightened excitement, the fear of the unexpected, the knowledge of an impending fight…all combined to put her fine elven senses on edge. The battle and her own labored breathing muffled her keen hearing, but she still heard the thrum of a vibrating string, followed by a whistle of feathers. She had run close to the source, and her cerulean eyes snapped to the branches shading the paths of

Cruso's and Urgosk's runs. Both warriors watched as something heavy dropped at their feet. The limp orc hit the ground and crushed its bow underneath. An arrow stood tall from its chest. Sir Cruso and Urgosk paused to consider the motionless form before glancing back over their shoulders.

The elf sorceress cracked a smile. "It appears Vallese has won your challenge."

Sir Cruso and Urgosk, both surprised, nodded in deference to the archer as she fitted another arrow in place on the run. While the other three continued forward, the elf glanced back for Mornik. The dwarf caught up a moment later, breathing heavily. She entertained the thought of how heavy his boots likely felt at that moment! As he reached the orc's body, Mornik gave it a redundant shot with his hammer.

"Now *that* rallies me!" He panted between breaths.

They hadn't advanced much farther before Sir Cruso held up a hand, signaling them to stop. He ran back toward his groupmates. Urgosk, on the other hand, paused but kept his hungry eyes forward.

"Why stop?" The half-orc called out.

The Diaran knight pointed back and forth across the area. "Look around! Get a feel for the battlefield!"

The others began looking around even as Mornik caught up once again. The dwarf breathed hard, spittle clinging to his beard. The rest were too intent on their surroundings.

Orcs were swarming the area. Fancifully colored orc warriors appeared, garbed in shreds of captured tunics and flags of past enemies. Some faces were smeared in blood - orc war paint. They appeared over the eastern hills, running toward the beach. Other than those that could be seen, many more were heard. The clash of weapons and sizzles of spellpower echoed right and left.

"The orcs have finally arrived in force…" Cruso started to say, but Allisee finished the thought. "We're spread all over, in small groups."

The stamping of many boots could be heard, and the party had only a small amount of time to react. Urgosk stepped into a clump of trees. Reaching to the flask at his neck, he took a quick swig of the hard-kicking concoction before gritting his teeth in an eager smile. Mornik whispered a quick prayer to Nandorrin. Flames erupted from the grass behind him and to the sides. Vallese reached two fingers into a belt pouch. Touching a tuft of fur kept in the bag, she intoned, "Panther spirit, grant me your boon." She felt the grace of a panther sweep through her body as she raised her bow.

Allisee transferred her staff to her left hand. Her right hand traced a pattern in the air as she intoned harsh syllables. Her right hand closed as if holding something, though she'd left her slender sword belted to her waist. Sir Cruso noted Urgosk picking an ambush spot. It was up to the knight to toe the line and hold the attention of whatever came into view. Hopefully the spellcaster and archer could inflict as much damage as possible while he held firm. The steel hand-and-a-half sword was already in his grip. He raised his shield for protection. "Dalios grant me strength of arm, Ganden forge me the shield of honor, and *The Codex* guide me on the righteous path."

*

The orcs came in clusters from different angles. They howled and screamed, touting all manner of crude weapons. Cruso could not impede them all alone. The knight knew only one phrase in the orc language. It had been taught to him as a boy in order that he might taunt his foes. He shouted it at the encroaching warriors, and several orcs changed course to come straight at him. Cruso knew what maneuver he would perform, but as he saw the multitude rushing at him, he feared he couldn't stop them all.

Vallese's arrow whistled by him, penetrating an orc's vital center and dropping him as he ran. The field on his left flared with a barrage of crackling electricity. Lightning forked between the ground and the air, reaching with its tendrils to throw orcs into fits of tremors.

As the first orc came into the knight's reach, it received a surprise. Cruso spun right, his shield slamming hard into the orc's side. This left the knight with his back facing the enemy, but with the shield still in the way. His sword, reversed to point downward, stabbed behind, surprising the orc formerly on his left side. Instead of getting in a vulnerable hit to Cruso, the orc received a point of steel through its guts. Cruso quickly reversed the motion, shield swinging to the left to deflect a jabbing spear from a third orc. The knight's blade chopped partway through the leg of the shield-slammed orc, dropping him. As Cruso shifted his sword grip and continued to block the spear jabs, his intuition made him kick backwards and struck an orc in the gut. The orc, knocked backward, rolled and came to rest in the path of Mornik's hammer.

The orcs missed seeing Urgosk as they charged in. The half-orc allowed the first one to run right by him. He stuck out his foot and tripped the second. Then he impaled a third with one of his javelins before the orc could properly realize the threat. Turning quickly, Urgosk turned to the first one and sent the bloody javelin flying at his back. The orc had its axe raised and likely believed it was about to cleave the dark-skinned archer. Instead, Vallese merely sidestepped as its pierced body hit the ground and rolled beyond. Her bow had been prepared to shoot it anyway; instead, she launched her shot and wounded a different orc near Urgosk.

The half-orc gripped his large axe with both hands and offered up a cry, "I'm of the First Hand!"

Urgosk stomped onto the tripped orc, hard enough to blast the air from him. The next orc in line yanked Vallese's arrow from its own flesh and threw it aside with a snarl. He swung a spiked club which Urgosk deflected. When Urgosk swung his axe, the wounded orc easily stepped aside…only to see the axe plant in the back of the tripped orc at Urgosk's feet instead. Not one to miss an opportunity, the upright orc jumped forward with club raised. Forsaking his stuck axe, Urgosk's fist landed an uppercut that put the orc out of the rest of the battle.

Allisee stood partly behind Cruso and off to Mornik's left, but nothing protected her from the orcs flanking around Cruso to get directly at her. Nevertheless, she had already dropped four of them with a spell she called "field of sparks." Cruso continued to hold the leading position against orcs trying to get past his shield, but the warrior would be in grave danger if she didn't keep clearing foes from his flank. The elf sorceress sent another wave of sparks forward. Her perceptive eyes and ears didn't miss the two orcs running well around her spell. They circled behind the group, and the orcs charged at Allisee when she turned towards them.

Allisee witnessed the orcs glancing to Mornik even as they ran toward her. Orcs hate dwarves most of all, and they clearly intended to have their fun with him. However, the field of fire surrounding Mornik's back denied them an easy attack…unless they took care of the irritating spellcaster.

Allisee dropped the staff aside and drew her sword. Her free hand weaved a pattern in the air. The orcs saw it, and they spread apart as they advanced. She only planned to target one. From her pointing finger, a bolt of energy caught one of the orcs. Its teeth gnashed and body shook as it dropped. The second one came upon her swinging a hooked sword. She evaded the first swing and, to her own surprise, managed to parry the second. Until the orc leveraged his curved weapon and yanked hers out of her grip. The two of them closed against each other in a tangle, though any who watched wasn't sure who grabbed whom. Together they fell and crashed into the brush.

Mornik saw the end of the exchange. Before he could do anything, he saw Allisee's former target staggering back to his feet, teeth chattering. The dwarf prayed to his god, forming a spell. The orc, perhaps still fearing he would die from her spell, charged madly at the dwarf despite the flames. Mornik completed his divine miracle, holding the pattern in his hand as he sidestepped the crazed orc. After the assailant stumbled through the flames and past the dwarf, the orc turned about in confusion.

"Oh, that flame doesn't actually burn," chuckled Mornik, indicating the fiery perimeter protecting his back. Then he held up his hand, so the orc could see a flaming chunk of coal settled there. The dwarf priest didn't appear to be hurt by its flame. "But this one does." The priest pitched the flaming coal at the orc, and it promptly torched him from head to foot.

Vallese drew an arrow, looking for a target. Not many opponents remained, but they all swarmed about Cruso and Urgosk. She alternated shots, first helping one, then the other. A spear-wielder harassed the knight; Cruso gasped as the spear managed to penetrate his side. Vallese put an arrow into the spearman's chest. Now freed to move, albeit unsteady, Cruso dispatched another troublesome orc. Switching back, Vallese shot an orc in the process of carving a scar into Urgosk's side.

Urgosk roared in rage! Spit flew from his lips as his lips curled into a sneer. His uneven fingernails dug claw-like into the dying orc's arm. Urgosk's anger invigorated him to throw his opponent aside, heedless of the new injury.

Mornik charged ahead with his hammer, calling to Vallese, "Archer, help our elf, she's in trouble."

Vallese swept her drawn bow across the area where she last saw Allisee. At first she saw no movement. A bloody figure arose from a thick band of brush. It took a moment to realize it was the elf, alive and apparently in no immediate danger.

"Stop the runners!" Sir Cruso yelled, arm holding his side as he stumbled to the ground.

Vallese turned back to the thick of the fight. Two orcs fled as fast as they could go. One didn't get far enough before Urgosk's second javelin speared it. The dusk-skinned archer sprang into motion. The spirit of the panther coursed through her. Her legs skipped across rocks and downed trees alike. Her eyes never left their focus on the lone runner, even as her feet propelled her past the spot where the latest victim breathed his last over the javelin embedded in him. Vallese landed on the perfect perch where she could view her prey free of obstructions. She launched her arrow, and it whistled across the wood until driving its steel head into the runner's heart.

*

The immediate area brewed quiet, but distant sounds of continuing skirmishes warned them the kettle would boil again soon. The wind heralded the clamor of battle from several directions. Mornik took the opportunity to see to their wounds. He glanced at the blood-covered elf first.

"I'm fine. This isn't mine." Allisee pulled a length of fabric from her pack and began scrubbing the blood off her arms.

Eyebrows raised, Mornik turned back to Cruso. The warrior's armor had a few new dents in it. Despite the protection, a blade managed to get through. Mornik praised Nandorrin as he channeled a divine miracle into the wound. Though it taxed Mornik's endurance, the divine aid coursed from his god to heal injuries. The bleeding stopped as regenerating skin closed over Cruso's wound.

Mornik ministered his injury while Sir Cruso observed Urgosk. The half-orc paced and growled, brimming with unreleased energy. The tusks gnashed and teeth ground together. The knight couldn't decide if Urgosk looked more angry or frustrated. He called out, "Urgosk?"

The half-orc threw a sneer his way, the yellow orbs threatened violence at the least provocation. He growled at the knight, as if he couldn't tell Cruso apart from the enemies they just killed. In that moment, Urgosk seemed as threatening to them as the native orcs. The half-orc forced his own eyes aside with a shake of his head, then resumed pacing.

Mornik spoke to Cruso as he inspected the success of his healing miracle. "Leave him be for now. Must be a berserker. Best to let him calm down on his own."

The knight's brow furrowed, "A berserker? What do you mean?"

"Sometimes he lets his rage take over when he fights." Mornik adopted an angry look as an example. "My people have fought orcs under the ground for as long as we have a history. Both dwarves and orcs see a lot of berserkers. If they let loose their rage in a fight, that anger gives them strength. They need time afterwards for their blood to cool down."

By the time Urgosk calmed down enough for the dwarf to check his wounds, he said, "Don't bother me when I'm like that. Won't end well."

Cruso looked around to check the group's condition. Allisee seemed to have given up trying to clean the mess on her. The elf retrieved both her staff and sword. Vallese, however, had taken an interest in Allisee's struggle. The archer walked over to the spot of the fight and was staring into the brush. Cruso walked over to join her.

Vallese's head turned, dark hair revealing red highlights under the bright sunlight. Her eyes opened wide in wonder as she pointed at what lie before her. "It's like animal tore it apart."

Cruso's jaw dropped. The orc had been raked by three parallel slash marks over a good portion of his torso. Vallese was right. It seemed as if something with a set of claws disemboweled it and slashed its throat. A lot of blood stained the ground underneath. The orc had died with a very surprised look frozen on its face. Both Cruso and Vallese peeked over their shoulders. Allisee had her back to them.

"Don't really know her well," Vallese whispered, "Do we?"

The knight waited until she looked back to his eyes, "I think we all have our share of secrets. Our journeys, motivations, fears, and nightmares are still unknown."

Just hearing the words 'fears' and 'nightmares' sent a chill along Vallese's arms. She reminded herself that the watching eyes from her nightmares were far away. The dark-skinned woman understood Cruso's point and merely nodded. They rejoined their companions without another word.

With the immediate threat handled, the group scanned the larger area. From the ridges to the east, down to the shoreline in the west, scattered pockets of fighting could be seen or heard. Orcs outnumbered the privateers, pushing the latter downhill toward the shoreline. Kashmer mariners were assembling ranks on the beach to form an organized line.

Sir Cruso took a step to the west, "Privateers will get cut off from the main force."

"And we'll be some of them." Allisee stated.

Even as she spoke, nearby orcs shouted in their guttural language. Urgosk looked a different direction than the others. He spotted something which put a devious glint in his eye as he turned back to the group.

He asked, "Can any of you hide us from view?" Both the elf sorceress and the dwarf priest raised their hands. "Good, how?"

"A mist, it will follow me as I move," The elf explained. "Enemies can see the mist, but we will be indistinct unless they get close. However, it won't grant me any special sight to see what lies beyond. I also can't cast other spells while maintaining it."

"Good enough," the half-orc smiled, tusks granting him a more devilish look than intended. He yanked a javelin from its victim. "We'll run inside the mist and get to safety. And you, dwarf?"

Mornik's hand immediately dropped. "If you plan to stay *inside* the mist, you'll want hers. Mine wouldn't be healthy for others."

Urgosk tossed a glance to the south. The companions could hear whooping and hollering approaching. "Cast your spell!"

They gathered close as Allisee spoke in an odd tongue. Mist began to swirl around their feet. As the rest waited for the spell's completion, an orc appeared from nearby trees. In one hand, it held a lit torch. Its presence in daylight seemed odd enough, until they watched the orc begin to touch the flames to an object in his other hand. It held a glass ball, its surface jutting spikes, and a pitch-soaked fuse dangling from the top. As the orc lit the fuse, Mornik stepped forward and shouted, "Rutan!"

To everyone's astonishment, especially the orc's, the flame took on a violent life of its own. It quickly blossomed to ten times its brightness and size. Fire licked at the fluid-filled glass ball, completely enveloped the length of the torch, and rushed down the arms of the orc. Surprised, the assailant dropped the glass ball upon the rocks at its feet. They heard the ball crack, and glimpsed the volatile fluid blossom into an inferno around the orc just as Allisee's mist finished coalescing around the group.

"Now, run with me!" Urgosk called out.

The half-orc ran through the haze. He would come to certain rocks or trees and suddenly change direction. He had planned his route before Allisee's mist blocked their vision. Sir Cruso began to lead the way alongside, but suddenly recalled the troubles the dwarf might have catching up. The mist was too thick to see Mornik. The knight stepped out of the way of the others and urged them onward.

Vallese appeared right behind him, rushing to keep the half-orc in sight. She uttered something that could have been a curse in her native language, followed by, "Urgosk! Where you going? This wrong way!"

Allisee rushed past, still holding aloft her hand and humming an odd pattern of sounds. The mist stayed centered on her as she moved, large enough to conceal the whole group. As Cruso looked about, he saw Mornik appearing from behind even as Vallese disappeared into the mist ahead. Hopefully Allisee could keep track of her and continue her spell. As Mornik drew near, another shadow charged in from behind.

"Low!" Cruso shouted. Mornik ducked his head as Cruso's sword flashed overhead. The orc took a serious hit, falling and rolling downhill. He was soon lost to the mist.

"Obliged," the dwarf huffed, still running.

Cruso heard Vallese call out, "What are you…" Her message paused in favor of the twang of her bowstring. "Beach is right! This wrong way!"

Cruso kept step with Mornik. He had no idea how Vallese or Urgosk could be sure of any direction. He barely saw Allisee's form running just ahead. The sorceress tripped, but managed to maintain both her stride and the humming syllables. On the ground lie a screaming orc bearing an arrow shaft in its gut. As before, Mornik took the time to aim a proper swing despite running. The screams ended abruptly. Both man and dwarf rushed around opposite ends of their fallen foe. A glance back from the knight revealed the body fading into the mist behind them. There were no immediate shadows in pursuit.

All of them had to rely on their ears since vision was so limited. More orc arrows whistled through the air. Ahead came the whoosh of steel and ripping of flesh. The rest of the party rushed by the headless orc Urgosk left in his wake. An arrow from behind barely missed Sir Cruso and deflected off Mornik's helmet.

Mornik spat out, "Sandstone!" A commonly-known dwarf curse.

The group fled sightlessly from the orcs' pursuit. They dodged trees, jumped ruts, and stumbled on loose pebbles. Their own breathing and heartbeats pounded their ears. One would stumble in the fog, then another would almost go down, but they kept their feet moving. The event seemed to last much longer than it probably did. Urgosk spoke in a hushed tone that managed to carry back to Cruso's ears. "Here! In there!"

They could hear Vallese's hesitation, "Crazy! Why?"

Cruso wished the archer had a wider understanding of their vocabulary, if only so that he might understand better what she protested. Quickly enough the rest of the group caught up to the arguing pair and could see Vallese's cause for alarm.

Urgosk indicated an orc cave as their escape route. Allisee couldn't talk without losing her spell. The elf pointed at the cave and vehemently shook her head. Mornik freely sounded his thoughts: "I'm feeling hammered over the anvil by all this running, and yer leading me into the nest?"

Urgosk pointed away from the cave. "Would you prefer standing in the open with these unorganized groups and the kidnappers of the Kashmer Navy?" The half-orc noticed Vallese hesitating at the entry. He slapped the dusky archer on her rump, urging her to enter. "I have a plan, but we have no time to talk."

Vallese spun about and glared at the half-orc. She held an arrow like a dagger ready to stab, but Urgosk had already turned to face the others. The rest stood frozen, undecided. Glances switched back and forth. Uncertainty wore on every visage. No one wanted to be the first to agree or argue. Urgosk, frustrated, raised his arms in exasperation and grunted.

Allisee, her voice still a slave to her spell, tapped Cruso on the arm. When he looked at her, she tilted her head towards the cave and motioned with her free arm for him to take the lead. He couldn't believe she was willing to take a chance on their unruly partner. Cruso sighed, readjusted his armor, and let his shield lead the way into the cave.

The elf would have followed, but the half-orc stopped her. "If you drop your spell, will the wind carry the mist away?"

She nodded. Urgosk said, "Drop your spell, then everyone get past the first turn in the cave and be quiet!"

Mornik and Vallese moved into the entry, both mumbling in their native tongues. Allisee stopped her chant and drew her thin sword with her former spell hand. Her cerulean eyes caught Urgosk's attention. "I'm trusting you. Please don't get us all killed."

He flashed a grin through his tusks. "Don't worry. Whatever happens, *I've* got a good chance of surviving the day."

Her lips pursed and nostrils flared, but she said no more. The wind began blowing their cover away. The elf slipped into the cave. Urgosk followed only a few steps before stopping. She glanced over her shoulder and saw him acting as sentry at the doorway. After following a turn in the tunnel, the passage widened into a small guardroom.

As Urgosk kept guard, he realized he hadn't performed his most sacred battle rite. Running his fingers along his blade, he sullied them with the blood of his opponents and smeared practiced trails of war paint across his cheeks and brow.

Orcs ran past the cave entry moments later, following the rolling mist as the breeze carried it along. At least one stopped to peer into the tunnel. Urgosk greeted him in the orc language, and he brandished his stained axe. Urgosk claimed he wounded one who tried to take cover there. The orc had little reason to question this orc-blood's account, even if he seemed to speak with a slight accent. After all, several orc tribes claimed these hills, though all had partnered to profit from their highborn hostage. Other orcs rushed by, howling for blood as they chased down the retreating fog. The curious orc proved eager to join in the slaughter. It ignored Urgosk and joined the chase. A few more bypassed the cave, none giving it more than a passing glance. The half-orc witnessed swarms of orcs descending the hills, pushing the Kashmer forces. Satisfied there were no immediate threats, Urgosk slipped down the tunnel to rejoin his group.

Volume 1, Chapter 5   "Cave Interlude"

Urgosk rounded the corner, and Vallese and Mornik immediately accosted him. Whatever complaints they started to voice cracked apart when they saw the grisly red adornment upon his face.

The half-orc spoke. "We would have had a hard fight just to make it back to Kashmer's Navy. Besides, we don't want to be trapped on the shore."

Allisee waved a hand at their groupmates, "They seem to think we're trapped *here*. I assume you have a plan?"

Urgosk nodded, "That Kashmer Navy, they're tryin' ta fight a standard rank-n-file war with a bunch of individuals. I heard tales from some privateers who fought at Stonelands. Stories they told made it sound like they got chewed up with those tactics. Even if they bull down this enemy, how are we supposed to earn the proper reward at the end?" He turned to face Cruso, noticing the knight crinkling his nose at the sight of the blood decorating his visage. "Would ya trust standin' shield ta shield with those other privateers on either side? Ya think they can hold a proper shield wall?"

"Nay," came the immediate answer, "but running down an orc hole doesn't seem bright."

"You think you can get us through," the elf interjected as statement. "So what happens if we delve deep into their territory and rescue the noble without allies to help us out, what then?"

Urgosk found it amusing that as shocked as their companions treated him for his warpaint, the elf stood practically covered in blood. "Ha-ra, ha-ra. If we get that far, hopefully we'll have figger'd it out by then. On the other hand, if an army comes over that last ridge, that highborn gonna be dead 'afore they get close. Nay reward fer anyone!"

Sir Cruso shrugged, "While I may disagree with your methods, I can't deny your thinking. You must have fooled the enemies at the cave entry?"

Urgosk nodded, though Mornik and Vallese practically grumbled. Allisee stood taller and declared, "If anyone has a better plan, it would be best if you shared it now."

The half-orc didn't miss the dwarf's glance at the cave entry. Urgosk warned him, "They're swarmin' out there."

Sir Cruso turned to Allisee, a thought on his mind, but his voice died upon seeing her eyes. In the dim light of the chamber, her blue eyes had vertical slits, like a cat. Having studied her eyes earlier, he knew they looked normal on the ship voyage. Cruso realized he was staring, and Allisee didn't miss his penetrating eyes. The elf cleared her throat. He averted his gaze, all memory of what he planned to say lost from his mind.

"For good or ill, the die is cast." As the elf waved her hand deeper into the passage, she looked at Urgosk. "Normally I like to do the negotiating, but I have a feeling you're our best bet to lead here. We'll try to stay a fair distance behind you."

"I'll be right behind to back you up if there is trouble." Cruso offered the half-orc.

Urgosk shook his head, "Yer not quiet. The sound of all that armor gives you away as human before they even see you. If we have a problem up front, I'll *axe* it to move aside." His tusks grinned.

"I suppose I'll guard the back," the knight resigned. He motioned between himself and Vallese. "Can we get a light source from our spellcasters?"

Urgosk began his trek down a tunnel barely lined with glowing moss and the occasional torch. For the most part, it remained very dark. "This is like home to me."

Cruso looked to the next person in line. Vallese had unstrung her bow in favor of arming herself with her staff. She addressed him, "You can't see? You must learn how to ask animals." She reached into a belt pouch, touching a feather inside it. "Owl, grant me your boon."

Vallese gave Urgosk a head start, then quietly stalked in his trail. The knight looked to the sorceress, assuming she would help him. Her cat-eyes blinked at him and she crept into the tunnel behind Vallese. Flustered, Cruso looked to his dwarf companion.

Mornik chuckled, "I think you are the only blind one here. Take this miracle." The priest made a prayer motion with one hand, uttering a dwarven word. "Donda."

A touch from Mornik placed a fire upon the middle of the knight's shield. Cruso felt heat, though it did not seem to burn as a normal fire. Nor did it harm his shield. Between the dwarf's miracle and the existing underground light, he felt he could manage. He took up his position in the rear as Mornik Heavyboot's loud steps preceded him.

*

Unlike his companions, Urgosk wasn't the least bit shaken traveling through orc tunnels. Everyone else in the group cast nervous looks at each shadowy corner they saw, and some jumped at distant noises echoing down the corridor. Vallese spent several minutes getting a feel for the half-orc's pace, trying to match it without drifting too close. The rest of the party didn't want to be visible if an enemy appeared. Urgosk suspected they'd normally have a harder time passing this way if it wasn't for every orc in the area massed on the surface to fight Kashmer. The young and noncombatant orcs were likely well-hidden in a deep lair.

The first time Vallese heard Urgosk talking to another orc, she tensed and flattened herself against a divot in the rough walls. The animal gift bestowed upon Vallese let her see and hear exceptionally well in the dark. Her own breath came loudly to her ears, but she tried to measure herself and listen. She could hear the occasional "ha-ra, ha-ra" from her companion. The entire conversation rambled in the orc language. A slight scuff against the floor startled her, but it was only Allisee.

Allisee seemed to be straining to hear the same conversation that Vallese heard clearly. The woman noticed the elf's cat-like eyes. She wondered if Allisee had a similar link to animals as she did. Firsthand experience taught Vallese that it seemed to be a rare gift.

Mornik and Cruso trailed the others, unaware of the conversation ahead. The knight noticed as Mornik suddenly flinched away from one of the walls as if something scared him. The dwarf priest gathered his wits and continued…hugging the opposite wall. When he reached the same spot, Cruso examined the wall Mornik had avoided. It was rough, but no cracks. A cobweb draped some of the divots in the wall. No writing or painted signs. He dared whisper to the dwarf, "What's wrong with the wall?"

Mornik turned away. Were his cheeks reddened? Cruso couldn't tell. The dwarf spoke, "Floor is just a little uneven there."

Cruso braced his feet across the tunnel, "I don't…"

"It's uneven!" Mornik hissed as he turned away. "I'm a dwarf, don't question me about stone."

Was Mornik (or dwarves) usually so defensive? The knight glanced once more at the wall. Only the small spider in its web stared back. Mornik and Cruso caught up to Vallese and Allisee, and the males' armor made it difficult to hear down the hall. Urgosk dropped back and told them it was clear, so they continued. Those first orcs he ran into were messengers moving along a cross-passage.

During the second encounter, Vallese heard a foreign voice shout at Urgosk, then nothing. A slight tap on the wall ahead served as the new signal that they could advance. The rest of the group crept by the body of an orc in elaborate headdress and necklaces. The latter of which had been discolored by the new opening in its neck. The rest of the group tensed. They imagined it wouldn't be long before someone found the corpse and raised an alarm. Urgosk left the body lying in a side passage. Hopefully that would help mislead others about the directions his murderers took.

The group was relieved when their course led to an exit. Urgosk left them in another antechamber while he scouted. A patchwork curtain obscured it from a larger pantry room, which had a crude door sealing it from the main passage. They noted supplies of all sorts jumbled around the room. A pair of unlit sconces hung on the walls, but the group didn't dare light them. Lacking the natural fungus in here, the only illumination came from the miracle placed upon Cruso's shield. Vallese restrung her bow and kept it pointed in the direction of the curtain. Similarly, Sir Cruso kept his steel hand-an-a-half sword at the ready.

Urgosk remained absent for some time. Footsteps could be heard passing down the main tunnel several times. In such times, the knight would press his shield face against the wall, muffling the miracle light. Occasionally, strange orc voices drifted to their ears. The four of them had no choice but to stand or sit in that cramped space. The group didn't dare utter idle conversation. The loudest noise they dared was the sound of their own breathing.

The outer door creaked open and shut, causing them all to tense. Vallese and Allisee detected steps just outside the curtain. With barely a warning, a grayish hand with broken nails yanked aside the curtain. Urgosk looked directly into Vallese's pointed arrow. The archer let out a tense breath and lowered her bow.

"Yer lookin' rather nervous there." He smiled.

From Sir Cruso to Mornik, they all looked ready to berate the half-orc but seemed too afraid to raise their voices. Allisee stepped forward first. Surprising the others, mostly Urgosk, she reached out and laid her hand softly upon his arm. Standing two inches taller than the orc, the elf nevertheless looked quite fragile even as she looked down and met his eyes.

"Aye, we're scared. All of us. I've put my faith in you. You may be playing this as if it's a fun game, but our lives are at great risk. If you feel as you did before about making time to laugh, then I'm asking you to wait until the risk is over. When we can return to a tavern and relax, I assure you, then we will all make a merry time of it!"

Urgosk's expression changed from amusement to seriousness. As the elf let go of his arm, he paused to draw in a breath before speaking.

"We have to cross an open area outside to git in to the next tunnel system. We'll be sneakin' through a low area to git into the tunnels under the next ridge. From what I've learned, it isn't used much. A clan built and abandoned it, but the main branch will take us where we need to be."

The others groaned at the idea of sneaking in the open.

"It's dark outside," Urgosk reassured them, "Storm clouds are gatherin' for the evenin'. In this twilight, y'all just be shapes in the gloom."

Vallese seemed in awe, "The day is ending?"

Urgosk shrugged, "Close enough, especially by the time we make some changes."

"What do you mean?" Mornik scowled at the orc.

A short time later, the party huddled near the tunnel's exit. The group looked different than how they entered the tunnel. This time each wore a skin or fur scavenged from the storeroom. Both the knight and the dwarf priest had tucked their shields across their backs and covered them. Urgosk continued briefing them on what to expect. They would be traversing a floodwater ravine. Small puddles of mud ran through it, and could suck at their steps. The majority of the orcs in the area were setting up defensive positions on higher ground. They were preparing in case Kashmer's forces got this far inland. Even at the cave exit, the ruckus of the orc forces drowned out any other noises. Axes chopped wood atop the steep ridge. Hammers knocked boards into place. Orc voices shouted orders. Forge-fires crackled sparks, some of which survived long enough to drift into the ravine. Cruso judged that a competent orc could hit him with a thrown rock. Luckily, the few orcs visible at the top edge of the ravine were distracted by their work.

Noting the peeking eyes of his companions drawn to the ridges, Urgosk whispered. "Glad yer gettin' through this area 'afore they finish it, eh?"

The knight tilted his head to the side, "As long as we don't get caught on the wrong side of it." Sir Cruso glanced at Allisee. "Is that fog still an option?"

Allisee met his gaze. Once again, he noted the vertical slits of her pupils. "A sorceress can draw from any of her tricks as long as she has strength, with some exceptions. I can give us more fog, but at the risk of not having the ability to cast my lightning if we are found."

The knight nodded, "Best if we are not found?"

The elf shook her head, adding "The orcs undoubtedly have magic-users of their own. If they see the fog, it may draw their attention."

Urgosk hefted a bundle of poles liberated from the storeroom. "Another reason to hide in plain sight. A few 'orcs' running bulky supplies from one tunnel to another won't catch a second glance at a distance."

The half-orc pointed across the ravine, to the location of the next tunnel entry. "At least that ridge is unoccupied. The further we run, the less likely someone will try to redirect us to the work uphill on this side."

The dwarf let loose a sigh, "I can hear my uncle now. 'What did you do in Kashmer, Mornik?' Oh, I ran into the wild hills and tried to pass as an orc."

As one, they hefted their "supplies" and stepped into the open. Sir Cruso felt vulnerable, knowing the surrounding orcs could see much better than he. He glanced at the ridge perched over the first cave network. A brutish orc stood there, slapping a club against one of the peons hauling supplies. The orc looked briefly at the new arrivals leaving the ravine. Urgosk caught it as well. He shouted at his party mates. By the manner he spoke, they assumed he was berating their progress. The half-orc went so far as to reach out and slap the stumbling dwarf. Mornik grumbled in return. The brute on the ridge resumed his attention on his own crew.

Raindrops fell as the first roll of thunder could be heard in the distance. The party struggled across the muck in the center of the channel. Floodwaters had carved a wide path, but a short jog would allow them to cross it easily.

Allisee dropped her basket. Urgosk, having to play his role for any onlookers, moved to berate her. She couldn't understand his words, but his meanings were clear as he pointed at the dropped items. Even as he indicated some, he subtly stepped on others, driving them into hiding under the mud. The elf was just getting her balance back and items in hand when Urgosk cuffed her on the head. Allisee's first reaction compelled her to straighten and stare him down. A second slap, stinging harder than the first, reminded her that a hostile audience wasn't far away. She meekly shrunk from him and resumed her passage. Vallese practically skipped past them both. The entire group watched her and wondered, not for the first time, what magic the woman possessed that gave her such unnatural grace.

They came within sight of an overhang. Urgosk's gestures indicated the entry to lie beneath a stone outcropping. The sky briefly illuminated the area, followed by more rumbling. As they drew within a few steps of a pile of mortared stones that formed a wall supporting the overhang, an orc stepped into view.

Only a few steps separated them. Their disguises would be no good from this close. The new orc called out some kind of greeting to Urgosk, who ran at the forefront. As the others stumbled to a stop from the shock, their half-orc companion put a hand to the flask hanging from his neck. A few words, and the new orc greedily stared at the offered flask. Then two more stepped from behind the wall.

"Athik? Athik!" One spoke in disbelief, pointing at Allisee's pale skin.

The air around Allisee hummed for a moment. Her hair seemed to rise and straighten suddenly. The orc facing her raised a cleaver. In that time, she stepped within his reach and laid a finger on his chain shirt.

Vallese dropped her load of poles…except one. Her staff jabbed forward, catching the second orc in the throat before he could shout. A quick spin, and the opposite end sent his brownish teeth flying.

Urgosk had less time to respond. He couldn't get his hands properly set on his axe handle before the other orc struck. It had been carrying an eating dirk, which it quickly planted into Urgosk's side. The half-orc dropped the axe. Urgosk fell into his berserk rage, latching both hands around the dirk-wielder's throat. The opponent's blade stabbed again, spraying more blood.

Lightning flashed next to them from the sorceress' finger, and Allisee's attacker was launched into the air, leaving his smoking, empty boots still standing in front of her. The limp, charred orc body bounced off the overhang before landing with splayed limbs on the ground.

Sir Cruso couldn't get a good grip on either sword due to his disguise. His last-resort weapon came into play. He used the parrying dagger from the back of his belt, and stabbed the dirk-wielding orc. Cruso's dagger pumped forth a couple more times, even as his target continued to jab a dirk into the half-orc. Urgosk let out a growl, flexing his strong arm muscles around the enemy's neck. A shake and a snap, and his attacker dropped. The body hit the ground with the head rolling loosely about the shoulders.

The last opponent lie there as Mornik finished what Vallese started. The warhammer Heel came crashing down, crushing bones. In all, the fight lasted only a couple breaths.

The dwarf glanced over his shoulder into the rainstorm. Confidant of no immediate threat, he turned back to the elf. "The lightning…"

"There is a storm." She said, even as a distant bolt lit the sky.

Urgosk sneered, roughly grabbing the nearest orc body. He paid no attention to his wounds, or perhaps his anger numbed him from the pain. His voice huffed with barely contained berserker rage, "We move these bodies into the tunnel! If they are spotted out here…"

His wounds overcame his resilience. Urgosk lost his grip as he collapsed. Mornik, who had been acting cautious around the berserker, rushed to his side. As the priest examined his injuries, Allisee surveyed the dead orcs.

"If we make it look like they fought each other…" Even as she spoke, Sir Cruso started dragging the orc bodies behind the mortared stone wall.

Vallese grabbed the bloodied dirk and placed it in the hands of a different orc. With luck, it would account for the stab wounds Sir Cruso inflicted. The knight continued to direct and transform a scene in which it would seem the orcs threw food and tankards at one another before coming to blows. He sighed at examining the blackened orc. Hopefully the orcs would think one of their own spellcasters was responsible.

Mornik channeled the fiery healing of Nandorrin into Urgosk's wounds. The bleeding stopped, wounds closed into scar tissue, then flaked away to reveal whole skin. The dwarf sat on his haunches. His face set in a tired grimace, the efforts of his miracle were plain to see. He looked pale, and his eyelids sagged as if from a lack of sleep. The half-orc stretched, looking revitalized. Urgosk offered only a silent nod of appreciation to the dwarf before rising up. He swayed a little, and Mornik steadied him.

The priest cautioned, "I can stop the loss of blood, but I can't replace it. You need rest."

Allisee glanced across the fire-lit ridge across the ravine. Despite her heightened vision, it was difficult to see if anyone was approaching. "Let's get into the tunnels and find a spot to recover."

*

Deep inside the cave tunnels, the group paused before a crude wooden door. In this case, 'door' proved to be a generous term for a set of loosely connected planks leaning against the passage. It wasn't wide enough to cover the side-tunnel extending behind it, though they noted it had orc writing scrawled across its surface. They perceived no lights or sounds coming from beyond.

"Here," Urgosk motioned, leaning against Sir Cruso for support. "This'll work well enough."

Vallese pointed her bow down the new tunnel. She moved quickly to explore it, but a cautionary hand from the sorceress stopped her. Allisee pointed to the crude letters and images painted on the door. "That looks to have some sort of warning tone. Am I right?"

The half-orc waved off the question. "It will be safe enough for us. The orcs here won't follow."

By that time, Mornik had a chance to examine the tunnel. The dwarf examined some cracks running along the walls. "This shifted, relatively recently. The area ahead may be at risk of collapsing. I know a bad tunnel when I see one."

"Maybe in a few years or decades," answered Urgosk. "Chances are it won't come down on us tonight. At least nay other orcs will venture beyond the warning sign."

"Safest den for now." Vallese reluctantly admitted.

"Break my forge!" The dwarf pounded his fist on the wall. His eyes fixed on the half-orc. "This situation just keeps sliding down-tunnel! Next predicament, you don't get to make the plans anymore!"

"I second," Allisee added. "But for now, I guess this will do."

Their archer resumed her scouting duties as they passed the door and advanced down the abandoned cave system. She kept an arrow ready for trouble. They entered a commons area that split into multiple levels and doorways. Even though Cruso was limited to the dancing flame Mornik had placed upon his shield, he had an idea of the open space due to distant light reflections and echoes. The party moved past several abandoned doorways.

"Nay go there!" Vallese pointed into the gloom.

"Aye, not safe." The elf looked about using her cat-like pupils. Allisee motioned in a new direction, "We can find shelter down this other hall, and still hear any pursuit with time to plan."

The half-orc roused his legs to action, but Cruso resisted the motion. "Wait, what is over there? My light doesn't go very far." He pointed in the dark direction Vallese had warned against.

The dwarf spit, "Cave collapsed."

Followed by Urgosk commenting, "Plus some bones. Rats are having a feast."

The knight decided he didn't need to know any more. The group ventured in the direction Allisee recommended, Urgosk hobbling beside Cruso. They settled into a chamber framed by artificial walls dividing the cave space. Some of the walls were only half-walls, segregating this area while allowing for possible interaction among the surrounding structures. With tired shrugs, they allowed packs to fall from shoulders and sat leaning against them. Weapons were put aside, but still within reach.

Mornik approached Urgosk. "Let's finish patching you."

The prayers of the Nandorrin priest flowed forth, allowing the miracle of health into the half-orc. Although the surface injuries had already been healed, Mornik's ministrations helped Urgosk breathe strong and deep. Mornik sat back heavily, "That's all I can do without getting some rest."

Sir Cruso pulled out a rag and cleaned the blood from his parrying dagger. Vallese counted the arrows left in her quiver. Allisee tipped her Traveler's Staff to one hand, summoning a nut-cake. Breaking the cake into two smaller portions, she handed one to her right and one to her left. Vallese, on her right, looked at the offering as if it jumped at her. She gingerly accepted it and took a bite. As a grin spread, she mumbled thanks through a mouthful of food.

On Allisee's left, Mornik accepted with less grace. The dwarf seemed less-than-pleased with the food choice. He narrowed his eyes at the elf and asked, "Are you sure?"

Allisee nodded, "It's very nourishing, but after a few years you tend to get tired of the taste. Please enjoy it."

The dwarf bowed his head briefly, "I have other plans, but thank you." He passed it on to Cruso, who accepted it most graciously.

The dwarf started digging through his pack as he spoke again, this time to all. "I know our situation is worrisome. We're sitting right in the middle of orc lands during a war. However, the more I get to know you folks, the more I feel confident I joined the right group. Your service to the privateers is quite commendable!"

"I nay privateer!"

As Vallese's sentence finished, Allisee responded. "Neither am I. I'm not here by choice."

The venom in both women's voices could be felt. Mornik stopped his pack-searching and his head popped up. "Kashmer only drafted privateers into service, alongside regular army and naval forces. You aren't a member of the privateers?"

The elf offered, "They cornered me outside *The Codex* monastery, once I had healed. They looked for privateers there. I told them I wasn't one. I even stated the obvious, that I wasn't from Kashmer. They said I was obviously an adventurer, membership or not, and told me I had to come. They gave me nay choice."

Mornik and Allisee both looked to Vallese, who barely held back her anger as she stumbled in the pacing and choice of her words. "I did not come to serve city. A gang of guards…pressed me into service. They insisted, 'Come with us or jail.' I only came here because everyone goes through Kashmer. All races and people. I only want to find home." She turned and pointed an accusing finger at the half-orc. "Now *you* drag me into orc-den. Going to get me dead."

The dwarf decided to turn the conversation before Urgosk could reply. "I'm truly sorry. I had nay idea the city forced folks into this fight. Is anyone else here a privateer?"

Cruso raised his hand, swallowing the last bit of nut-cake as he did. "I joined. Best place to find work for a cast-out knight."

"Cast-out?" Allisee and Urgosk said, practically in unison.

Cruso winced, "A story for another time, perhaps. Anyway, once I joined the privateers I set out looking to fit in. That's when I found trouble in the sewers and rushed to help." He glanced to Mornik, "And you saved me."

Finished with his explanation, all eyes shifted to Urgosk. The half-orc smirked, then paused long enough to take a deep draw from a flask. "I was at the privateer quest crier, plannin' ta ask them about the membership. Then, the Kashmer guards showed up. I saw trouble comin' and signed up rather than be arrested."

The others could see the open-mouthed shock on Mornik's face. The dwarf sputtered, "I had nay idea! The audacity! So most of you were given nay choice?" As the others shook their heads and confirmed their stories, Heavyboot pounded his fist into his other palm a few times. "A fine way to lose a war. Throwing forced conscripts, like fodder, into the front line!"

The elf put up a restraining hand. "A bad idea, to be true, but I have faith in all of you." Silently, she thought, *They have to believe in each other, or we won't survive this crazy gambit.*

The sorceress cradled her traveler's staff. "I can imbue this staff with one spell for the day. Saves my energy for later. I'll imbue it with the mist I used to cover us when we ran into the cave system."

Mornik looked up, "Why not add more lightening to it?"

She answered, "By using the staff to power the spell, it frees up my voice."

Allisee turned her face to include Vallese, who visibly fumed at their orc-blood companion, before saying, "We probably should rest for a bit, and make better plans for crossing the next ravine."

Silence descended on their conversation until Cruso got to his feet. "Allisee is correct. We need rest, and who knows when we'll get another chance? We're dependent on ourselves, so sleep and eat while you have the chance."

Urgosk glanced up, "Where are you going?"

"Going back down the tunnel as far as I dare without light. I'll keep my ears out in case anyone comes searching."

As Cruso reclaimed his sword, Allisee stood up, holding her backpack of multi-colored, stitched hides. "I relish the chance to freshen up. A change of clothes is overdue."

The others snuck glances at the elf's bloodied garments. Red stains trailed from arms across torso and down her legs. Sir Cruso and Vallese couldn't shake the memory of the torn orc that had tackled Allisee.

"Excuse me," Allisee remarked, as she strode to a nearby structure. Full walls separated the view from the camp, so she went behind it to clean up.

Vallese, shrugging and unconcerned, started unstrapping her armor. By the time Cruso had disappeared into the dark, the archer began removing her tunic as well. The now-topless female apparently didn't care about the two men still present. She even let out a nut-cake inspired burp, without trying to stifle it or asking pardon. As she continued to strip, red-faced Mornik turned away out of respect. As he did, he noticed Urgosk leering at the woman, enjoying his flask.

"Turn your eyes away out of respect!"

The elf, overhearing the dwarf's words, peeked out from the other structure. She glanced at Vallese's nudity, assessed Urgosk and Mornik's reactions, and called out, "Vallese! Come over here with your things!"

The archer tilted her head as she looked to the sorceress. "Why?"

"Because Urgosk looks hungry, and he's sizing you up as the meal!"

Vallese turned, finally realizing Urgosk's leer and Mornik's uncomfortable aversion of his head. Alarmed, she gathered her armor, weapons, and clothing then hurried behind the wall with the sorceress. Allisee, similarly undressed, was using a wet cloth and enticingly scented soaps to cleanse herself. She handed a spare cloth and the soap to Vallese.

"People uncomfortable with other bodies?" Vallese pieced together the reactions of her companions. The woman sniffed at the scented soap, savoring the aroma.

"It is inappropriate for women and men to be naked for the other gender, unless married or moving on to sex. Between the same gender there's no issue."

"Gender?"

"Gender means whether you are man or woman."

Vallese closed her eyes and smiled, enjoying the scent of the soap as she started washing. "What is that word…inappropriate?"

The elf paused, "It means: not accepted as custom. Typically, outside of elf lands, getting naked around men is a prelude…" Allisee realized the human likely didn't know 'prelude' either. "It can mean you want sex, even though you don't."

Vallese, eyes closed, didn't see the elf's reaction as she answered. "Well, if the men needed…their release, I would submit like always. Except that tusk-tooth! I would fight him!"

Wide-eyed and frozen, Allisee repeated those words in her mind. *I would submit like always.* The elf paused and stared, but Vallese continued unaware. Without knowing it, the woman touched on a sore subject from Allisee's heritage. The elf gave Vallese a second look, taking in formerly hidden details. Vallese's curves were pronounced in all the right places where men look. Of course, she'd already seen the splotchy, spotted tattoos around the woman's shoulders, upper arms, and ringing her ankles. However, by undressing, Vallese had set aside some cloth wraps that revealed something new in her upper forearms and front of her elbow. Multiple, small scars deformed the skin in those areas. Scratches? Repeated punctures? Allisee wondered if Vallese's arm wraps were solely to cover those scars. She decided to try finding a way to probe more of this woman's history.

Allisee admitted to herself that her own life quest had a tendency to distract her from the trials of others. She resolved to learn more about this young woman. "Can you repeat those words you spoke to Urgosk on the boat? The words from your homeland tongue?"

Vallese glanced up from scrubbing, taking a moment to recall her words. She repeated them as best she could. The language was much different than the local human's Hespal language. She clicked her tongue against her teeth several times. Once finished, Vallese waited while Allisee tried to mimic the mouth movements and some of the sounds.

After a minute, the elf spoke, "You were insulting him? You said something bad about his morals or behavior?"

Vallese's eyes widened, "You know my words?!"

Shaking her head, Allisee replied, "I've been told I have a gift with languages. I understand them on a level that few can match. I could likely learn your language in a short time. Well, if we survive to get the chance."

Vallese grinned, "We start some now. This is how I say hello…"

While the women acquainted themselves better, Urgosk posed a question to Mornik as the dwarf rummaged through a bag. "Sate my curiosity. Why's a dwarf travelin' human lands, joinin' the privateers of his own wishes?"

"I'm on a pilgrimage…of sorts. I have subjects I wish to research…ah, there it is!" The dwarf withdrew a paper-like wrap from his pack, pulling out two small, bread-like loaves. He began to wrap the remainder and return them. "The privateers are a diverse group. They travel far and discover much. I thought it would be a good organization in which to learn what I need. Here, have one of these."

The dwarf put one lump in Urgosk's hand. It seemed a type of hard biscuit, marked with a splotchy variety of colors. The half-orc sniffed at it. He detected an earthy scent. "What is it?"

Mornik grinned. "Nom." The dwarf took a bite out of his loaf.

Keeping one eye on the priest, Urgosk sank his tusks into the biscuit. Indeed, it was a hard biscuit meant for travel nourishment. He chewed it slowly, noticing the dwarf sitting on edge. Mornik seemed to have more than a passing interest in Urgosk's opinion. The half-orc had the brief urge to feign being poisoned, but he let the temptation pass. Both ravished the loaves as they talked.

He shrugged. "Fillin', but lacks taste. Any meat in it?"

Mornik chuckled, "Nay, but I plan to try someday. However, a meat version won't keep well on the road. That's why I carry salted meat strips as well."

At that, the half-orc's head perked up. Mornik didn't have to wait for him to ask the next question. "I'm saving the meat strips for the morning. Start the day with some kick. I might share, but only for cooperative folks who don't stir up trouble." The dwarf threw a stern look at Urgosk.

A sudden thought entered Urgosk's head. "Wait, what *is* nom made from?"

"Various plants and mold from the Deeprealm." Urgosk's face went sour, but Mornik continued. "Depending what you use, the taste varies. I consider it a hobby. I'd like to find the best recipe I can someday and sell the secret."

Urgosk decided it would be the best meal he would get, since he brought nothing. "So, yer pilgrimage is about cookin'?"

"Nay, but my travels should also benefit my attempts at cooking and brewing."

Urgosk nearly jumped up. "Tell me ya brought some swill!"

Chuckling, Mornik replied. "Nay. But if you help keep me alive until we return to Kashmer, I'll buy a round."

Settling back down, the half-orc added, "How is yer pilgrimage goin' so far?"

The dwarf sighed, "I'm trapped in dangerous lands, not a single bit of research material in sight, sharing a meal with an orc." He shrugged. "Not how I foresaw things when I left home."

By the time Urgosk finished the biscuit, his body felt like lead and the exertions of the day made him lie down. The women returned, and neither of the two males could believe the change in Allisee. Aside from being clean, she gave off a scent like woodland flowers. Her dress looked functional for movement, yet would be considered more formal than stealthy orc-hunting dictated. They all settled down to get what little rest they could.

While their eyelids grew heavy, they heard the priest intoning an evening prayer. A part of his message reflected the adventures of the day, though his companions proved too weary to recall much of his words.

Mornik ended his prayer, "…and please oversee the safety of your servant, through the cold hours of the night, until the dawn stokes the fires anew."

Volume 1, Chapter 6   **"Into the Heart"**

Enhanced by her animal link, Vallese's senses picked up the sounds of her companions rising from their rest. Keeping a watch out for any orcs, she hid in the spot she had relieved Sir Cruso from hours earlier. Through the night, only occasional exclamations could be heard from the orc tunnels. None seemed close. It allowed Vallese a lot of time to think about her homeland. She retained precious few memories. Her hand would often drift unconsciously to the spirit pouch hanging from her neck. She didn't understand the significance of any of the pieces within, though she could guess one. A tiny vial of dirt. Whatever it was supposed to represent, it contained a piece of home. When she found that scent again, she would be on her tribal lands. Vallese spent much of the watch dwelling on the past. Despite her heightened senses, she didn't hear Urgosk sneaking up from behind until too late. She half-turned at a sound just as the half-orc's brownish-gray hand slapped her bottom as he rushed along.

"Scoutin' darlin', don't shoot me!"

In a language only Allisee had a chance to decipher, Vallese cursed and insulted him as he disappeared. In the darkness leading up to that event, Vallese had examined her feelings over her situation: conscripted by a foreign city, pulled away from her life's quest, forced into a war, and now trapped in enemy lands. She almost convinced herself she was angrier at her situation rather than the half-orc's involvement in it. Urgosk's passing slap elevated him back to the most vexing spot on her list. Vallese felt no closer to home, and no farther than from where she had escaped. Her course felt uncertain. At least the elf had reached out to her. She would be more than willing to align her course to Allisee's fate, even as each woman sorted out her own journey.

And yet, she hadn't gotten the courage to ask the sorceress how that orc victim had become so completely torn and disemboweled. Maybe she wasn't ready for that answer?

When Allisee appeared, offering Vallese a rest, the archer decided she still wasn't ready for an answer. Looking over the elf, she instead asked, "Did you get your rest?"

The elf nodded, "I'm fine. You haven't gotten any food yet, have you? Mornik spiced up Kashmer's rations. Might as well get something before we move."

Vallese accepted. Meager as morningfest was, it sated her. The conversation needed the most improvement. Mornik and Sir Cruso discussed gods and religion. Many unfamiliar words went beyond her understanding. She paid them little heed. She understood enough that Mornik worshipped a god of fire and…whatever a forge meant. Sir Cruso prayed to several gods, but favored none. She knew his guidance came from a 'Codex' book that he carried. Vallese had no use for gods, since none ever seemed to help her.

*

Hours later, all five felt vulnerable once under the open sky. Clouds shrouded the daytime sun, and it proved difficult to guess the exact time of day. Urgosk led them uphill, following a narrow, hidden trail. The half-orc made the most of the terrain, guiding them higher and higher while still keeping a ridge on one side and thick woods on the other. They saw no orcs, but heard voices. Smoke brought the scent of something burning. Cookfires? Something more sinister?

Urgosk waved them to a stop. "Wait."

He disappeared further up the trail without another word. Heartbeats passed as the group hunkered in a low spot. A vocal noise, barely a syllable, sounded but then stopped as if cut short. Urgosk returned. The others witnessed fresh war paint of blood adorning his face.

"It's clear. Stay low, we'll get a good view up there."

The rest fell in line. They found a campsite at the crest of the hill. Boulders and shrubs offered good cover, while orc-made, narrow trails offered scouts easy access all around the top. Orcs used it as a lookout. Only two could be seen, and wet blood still pooled in their fatal wounds.

"That won't stay undiscovered for long," Allisee pointed out.

"Hopefully long enough, 'sides, the view's worth it."

Urgosk indicated a view on the north side of the hill. He pointed westward first, "Kashmer's Navy and the other privateers are that way." They looked and saw distant smoke plumes.

He panned to the right. They saw endless rolling hills and brush. Several hills were capped with camps, cookfires, banners, and lookout towers. As he finally swept around to the east, they could see signs of several angry fires throwing smoke over the whole landscape. As they watched, a distant siege weapon fired, throwing a fiery mass eastward.

"And somewhere in that firestorm is Kashmer's Army, hammerin' from the other side. Some orcs told me Kashmer is attackin' a fortress called Dundrol. They also said its where a tribe holds that noble hostage."

The elf mused, "Hoping to still use him as a bargaining chip?"

Sir Cruso asked, "I wonder why they don't move him further from the fighting?"

"Nay unified nation," Urgosk extended his arms to encompass the various camps on the horizon, "They live separate and tribal, even with an enemy knockin'. The orcs holding Dundrol captured the human, so Dundrol is where he'll stay. Until they execute him rather than give him up."

"Closer to army than navy," Vallese observed.

"And the army lies beyond all that fighting." Mornik finished. "Whatever is going on down there is letting off a good amount of fire and destruction. Approaching that stronghold won't be easy."

The half-orc shrugged, "Nay, but they are looking the other direction."

They stared to the east, trying in vain to make out the details of the fortress. Smoke and terrain obscured much of it. They could see no tall walls or parapets. Some buildings, which were more like mortared piles of rocks, rose from different points of the area.

Urgosk answered many of their unspoken questions. "Most of the fortress is likely underground. Caves give more shelter than walls. Findin' a way over a wall would be easy, if that tribe isn't lookin'. The noble is likely in the cave system, which is not so easy."

Cruso's steel hand-an-a-half sword swung a bit as he tested its weight. "There is nay means to get down there without a fight."

Urgosk hmphed, "Since we must fight…we might as well grab the noble and reward on the way through."

The knight scowled at the half-orc. "Flawless logic, I am sure."

Vallese crossed her arms. "Don't need reward. Don't need land next to Kashmer!"

"Oh, we'll get land," the dwarf demonstrated with his hands. "We'll get a plot six feet deep or a spot behind a stone cover in a catacomb."

The elf called upon them all. "We can plan all we want, but the safety of Kashmer's forces lies in that direction. Somehow, we must get through. If the opportunity provides a chance of rescue, we should accept it. However we feel about this situation, any firm plans we make will be cast aside the moment the fighting starts. When that happens, everything is reflex and capabilities."

As Allisee, Vallese and Mornik scanned the hill's descent, Urgosk felt a hand grab his arm. "A moment please," Cruso said with a hint of steel in his voice.

The knight's grip insistently pulled Urgosk aside. He decided not to resist, interested as he was in whatever the knight required. The others noted the interaction, but decided to focus ahead while the two warriors sought privacy.

Once they seemed to have enough distance from the others, Urgosk grinned and dared, "'Ave enough stomach fer this fight?"

"For myself? Of course!" Sir Cruso snorted. "From birth, I was bred for warfare. Reward or nay, I would still be out here, fighting this foe, attempting the rescue. Wouldn't be my first quest! Dalios grants me the strength of arm to sunder foes with my sword. Ganden forged my shield from the embodiment of honor. *The Codex* guides me on the righteous path. Honor is everything, Valor a close second."

The half-orc scrunched his face and stuck a finger in his ear. Wiggling loose a fair amount of ear wax, he commented. "I think ya already gave part of that speech 'afore. What of it?"

"By myself or partnered with you, I would gladly charge and lay down my life for the quest." Sir Cruso leaned to one side, subtly extending a pointed finger. "The women didn't ask for this. They were forced along. Nay rescue is worth it if an innocent gets killed."

Urgosk shrugged, "That yer chivalry talking? I don't think those women are that innocent. Particularly the way Sticks dresses."

"Sticks?"

Urgosk nodded at Vallese. The woman seemed to be keeping her head half-turned to the men's conversation, despite being over sixty feet away. "Bow, arrows, staff...Sticks."

The half-orc couldn't see it, but she threw a glare in his direction before turning her head away. Sir Cruso resolved that any further "private" discussions should be held at an even farther distance apart.

"Why are you saddling her with a nickname?"

The half-orc responded with a solid finger-jab into Cruso's breastplate. "In the First Hand, a warrior's name was meaningless. We all earned our nicknames, and lived by how others viewed us. I nickname all my companions."

The knight reached a hand up and rubbed at his temple. "Why pick names for us now? When did you make this choice?"

Urgosk shrugged, "Ya had to earn 'em first. I had to know ya by yer actions."

Despite his better judgment, the knight felt compelled to ask. "What is my nickname?"

"Paladin."

Cruso's eyes narrowed, "Paladins channel divine miracles from their deities. I'm nay paladin."

One of the half-orc's eyebrows raised. "Could've fooled me."

Cruso shook his head. Taking a moment to recall their conversation, before the topic of nicknames altered the subject, he replied. "Maybe it is chivalry which burdens me with concern for the women; however, you can't deny they were forced here against their will. Whatever happens in our rescue of the noble, we have a duty to see them safely through this."

Tired of the conversation, Urgosk raised his right hand. "I'll help 'em safely through this, or endure a beatin' on their behalf."

As they returned to the group, Allisee looked inquisitively at both, "If you two have worked out whatever you needed, we should move onward."

The warriors nodded. The group took in one last look at the terrain ahead, trying to memorize the valleys and hills. Beyond that, the fog of battle sat beside their destination.

*

The five of them clambered a crooked path to the base of the hill. A distant observer might have mistaken them for five orcs. They continued with disguises, though not as complete as the ones they first used. Cruso and Mornik complained they couldn't draw a weapon properly in their original ruse. This time all but Urgosk settled for orc-borrowed cloaks and ugly cloth wrappings around their footwear. Both Mornik and Cruso also used abandoned sacks decorated by the orcs to cover the emblems on their shields.

"Through here, let's use this lane." Urgosk prompted.

The sorceress cursed as long thorns ripped at her new garb. "Are these for food or protection?"

"Both," the half-orc's tone revealed his admiration as he grabbed and savored some berries. "Good plan, eh?"

Lines of sharp brambles followed the contours and bends at the base of the hills, effectively walling off anyone from crossing them except at designated points. Trails ran between the rows of thorns, and ripe, orange-red berries hung in groups from the branches. The group ran through pathways cutting through the low valleys, lifting their eyes to the sides in search of other potential watchers. Brambles stretched endlessly to each side, with only a few breaks. The air held some smoke, blown across the hills from the spot at which Kashmer's army fought.

Vallese admired the orcs' planning. The orc tribes built a formidable defense in case any invaders pressed this far. She picked and gulped a few berries as she ran. They were tasty, but they also rekindled a memory: an old woman, skin as dark as hers, rubbing a berry against her lips. Try as she might, Vallese couldn't recall anything more than that faint image.

Footsteps echoed from ahead, around a slight bend.

Urgosk waved a hand for the others to stop. Without waiting to see their reaction, the half-orc kicked his pace into a run. The group had nowhere to hide. Brambles corralled them on both sides as rising hills blocked any easy retreat from the path.

Urgosk called out in his language. One voice yelled back. The half-orc companion uttered a longer sentence. Vallese placed an arrow and drew her bow. Mornik pulled forth a charm from a neck chain, hidden under layers of beard hair. He whispered words of prayer into it.

Their half-orc companion rounded a bend, moving out of their sight. Urgosk and the unseen orc exchanged words at a rapid pace. However, the foot falls kept drawing near. A moment later, the still-talking enemy rounded the bend. His words and feet stopped abruptly as he saw the group.

One of Urgosk's javelins flew into his back about the same time as Vallese's arrow punched through his chest. Unable to draw breath or scream, the orc dropped dead.

Everyone regrouped at the body. The sorceress caught Urgosk's attention. "Why didn't you kill him before he saw us? He might have gotten off a warning shout."

"This was a runner, runnin' a message…"

Before Urgosk could finish, Sir Cruso knelt at the body and started searching it. The knight rummaged for bags or satchels of any kind. The half-orc interrupted him.

"Nay, soldier of Diara, ya won't find a written message in a pack or such. His words carried the message, so I had to ask nicely. He was still talking when we killed him. He said Dundrol is closin' their surface hatches. The humans are pushin' too close. Any reinforcements should enter through the mill entrance."

Mornik tilted his head as he asked, "They have a mill?"

Urgosk gave his embedded javelin a further twist before yanking it from the corpse. "We aren't the savages you think. A good mill on a good river provides crafted weapons, grinding flour, building materials and might even be needed for ale! Brings a lot of prestige to the tribe."

Sir Cruso wrinkled his nose as he glanced at Urgosk. "Orc prestige?"

Urgosk shrugged, "Closest meanin' that comes to mind. Words have more weight at war councils, smaller tribes more willin' to put yer banner over theirs, other tribes want nay trouble with ya."

"How far?" Allisee interrupted.

He shrugged, "Nay idea. But we're headed the right way."

Cruso and Urgosk hefted the body, throwing it over the line of brambles. They could do nothing else to hide it. With few words exchanged, they all quickened their pace. Each shared the sudden apprehension that time worked against them. Around two more hills they traveled, bordered by the thorns or steep rocks. The smell of burning wood filled the air. Occasionally smoke left a haze, but it never became thick. The trail opened slightly, so that a wagon might barely pass between the bramble lines. The party still had to navigate rocks and muddy depressions along the path.

"Arrow!" Vallese called.

No sooner than her call, the rest of the group heard more than one shaft whistling. A slight stutter-step from the woman kept her just out of harm's way. Another arrow, aimed for Cruso's head, clipped the helm hidden under the orc cloak. Mornik raised his shield in time for it to catch a third. Before they recovered from the surprise, they heard the call.

A horn blasted several quick notes from the hill to one side. The opposite side blew a horn in response. Orc voices raised from every direction. They whooped and hollered at finding prey. Weapons thumped against shields.

"Rocks!" The dwarf cursed.

Despite the word being a common dwarf curse, Urgosk and Allisee hunched lower as they ran and scanned the sky for thrown boulders. Although there were no rocks dropping, the incoming arrows concerned them enough. Vallese returned a shot, but more answered back. Cruso started to reach for the folded crossbow hanging on his back, then apparently thought differently. "There's nay cover here!"

As the knight ran onward, he noted breaks in the brambles ahead. Any charging orcs would be able to access the path easily.

Allisee declared, "I'll make cover, now run!"

The sorceress brought forth her traveling staff. As Allisee had declared the previous evening, she could power her fog through the staff, freeing her voice for the duration. The mist rapidly spread out and covered the group. Allisee followed that by grabbing her wand briefly, expelling a charge from it to power a protective barrier around herself.

The five of them ran along the ravine. More horn calls joined the first two, though some were distant. A fast-pounding drum gave them a cadence with which to set their own frantic pace. Orc voices carried the majority of the noise. They let loose war cries and could be heard stumbling down the hill. Urgosk and Cruso drew weapons even as both charged. The knight gave a nod to the half-orc; the gesture returned by a yellow display of teeth.

"Not too fast," the elf warned, "Our healer has short legs."

"I have…encouragement…to keep up!" He huffed as he ran.

Arrows whistled through the fog. Vallese set her bow to rest over her shoulders, unslinging her staff. She dropped back, offering the priest some protection in case anything threatened him.

The first orc to arrive through the fog appeared to the side, coming in behind Cruso. Its red eyes focused on the elf. By the time Cruso came to a stop, the orc was within weapon's reach. Allisee didn't let it get closer. She raised her free arm, barking an arcane command. A bolt of energy flashed. The spell left the orc convulsing on the trail as Allisee ran by it. As before, Heavyboot delivered a blow with Heel.

Cruso resumed his charge a few steps behind Urgosk. The half-orc paused to throw a javelin at a shadow emerging three meters away. Struck in the gut, the attacker stumbled the last steps and dropped into a kneeling position near Urgosk. The orc writhed, clutching his injury as the javelin haft propped him upright. An arrow from mist caught Urgosk in his leathers, drawing a growl from him. Urgosk yanked the arrow free, ran around the kneeling opponent, then stabbed the arrow into another orc wielding a bow. Cruso delivered a one-handed slice of his sword to finish the javelin-wounded orc. His shield rose in time to deflect a thrown spear. As the newest enemy stepped from the fog, Cruso cut through him before he could get another weapon into play.

In the back of the party, Vallese and Mornik turned heads as they spotted a form emerging from the fog. "Mine! Run!" She called out. Silently adding, *I am the panther*, as she touched a piece of fur in her pocket.

An orc arrow zipped harmlessly between her and her opponent. Mornik kept pumping his legs at a run. Vallese's staff came down, deflecting the head of a stabbing spear. She two-handedly jabbed the staff crosswise, smashing her opponent's nose with the middle of the staff. Without breaking her momentum, she spun one end around and rapped his skull. He kissed the dirt. Vallese resumed her stride next to Mornik.

The shabby orc cloaks worn by the party were not enough to make the orcs pause in their attacks. One cloak after another got discarded by the party members as they decided to get them out of the way. The sackcloth covering Cruso's shield was ripped away by an orc's axe before the knight separated its leg and left the enemy writhing. Heel scored another hit a moment later.

A wave of arrows pierced the fog from their right side. One bounced off Cruso's armor, another deflected from Allisee's barrier. After they heard the bowstring twangs, the sound changed to approaching battle cries. Urgosk and Cruso veered in that direction. Mornik set his hammer into its belt-ring, prepared to use his free hand to channel any needed miracle. The companions could make out a break in the brambles and the wave of orcs rushing through it. The small tide rolled at them from the side, stretching farther than Cruso and Urgosk could block.

One threw itself upon Allisee even as she raised her hand against it. A wickedly curved axe descended at her arm. The blade bounced off Allisee's invisible barrier, yet struck hard enough to knock her down and lose the staff from her hand.

"Allisee!" Vallese cried out, but a closing enemy kept her busy.

Disoriented, the elf tried getting back to her feet as her opponent delivered a second axe blow. Again, the blade pushed at her but couldn't slice through the barrier. In frustration, the orc kicked her ribs. This time, the attack went through the depleted spell.

A piece of coal, set aflame, flew at the orc as he lined up his axe for the finishing blow. A moment later, the enemy became a pillar of flame. It screamed and fell aside. Mornik put a hand on Allisee, eliciting a whimper from her as he touched her broken ribs. She coughed, her blood speckling the trail.

"We'll get that cough sorted." He began his revival prayer to mend her wounds.

Allisee felt the healing fires of the dwarf re-forge her ribs. The coughing continued, unabated. Mornik wouldn't understand, but how could he? It wasn't just the injury from the orc's parting kick. The elf felt this sensation before, in times of duress. She felt a pressure well up from her insides. Heartburn tore at her throat. A heaving sensation rippled through her torso. It felt like her body wanted to vomit, but nothing ever came. Instead, pinpoint shocks made her mouth bleed. The dwarf's miracle healed the damage, but there was little she could do until the waves of this familiar feeling ran their course. Her churning insides weren't directly related to the injury from the kick. She knew the cause originated her curse. Just as her nightmares revealed, it heralded her destiny to become a monster. Something inside wanted to break free and consume her.

"The fog!" Cruso yelled.

The waves of pressure running through Allisee subsided. As she struggled to rise, the elf realized her concentration had lapsed. The cloud dispersed, making them more vulnerable. Vallese, an opponent dead near her, stood protectively before her and the dwarf. The dwarf's shield lie near the archer's legs as she worked her bow. Her quiver held only a few arrows as she exchanged fire with the orcs. Glancing a different direction, Allisee noted Cruso and Urgosk teaming up on a retreating opponent. Both her wounded allies dripped blood, some of it landing on the severed limbs at their feet.

"We have to move," she urged. "Time works against us."

Mornik retrieved his shield. More orcs offered threats in the forms of foreign insults and shaking weapons. However, the remaining orcs stood just beyond the bramble gaps on either side of the group. At least for the moment, they stayed several paces away from the reach of a sword. Allisee retrieved her staff. At her command, the staff shrunk down to the size of a wand. She tucked it into her pack. Cruso began to lead the way, but Urgosk only got a few more steps before faltering to one knee. The priest came to his side in an instant.

Cruso yelled to the half-orc, "You need to get some real armor to stand toe-to-toe."

As Mornik administered the healing miracle, several more orcs lunged forward. The knight faced combat before the half-orc could reply. He stood firm against three. The enemies had a hard time trying to find a weak spot in the armor, but they had managed to dent it in a few places. He couldn't block all their blows, and didn't attempt to do so.

As the dwarf's healing miracle came to a close, Urgosk had his flask to his lips. He downed a swig and shoved the cork back in place. "The more they hurt me, the more I get mad."

He flew from Mornik's touch howling in a berserk rage. Urgosk sprinted at Cruso's shield-side enemy, but dropped into a sliding kick. The opponent fell as the half-orc skidded through his legs and rolled upright. Urgosk's spiked axe whooshed around, chopping a fourth orc that had just arrived. It distracted the middle orc confronting the knight. A fatal error. The hand-and-a-half blade took its head before engaging the last standing orc. Urgosk turned to deal with the tripped opponent.

The two warriors failed to stop another group from flanking the party. Mornik raised shield and hammer against a similarly armed, taller foe. Vallese switched back to her staff as others closed in. The archer cast a worried glance at the sorceress. Allisee moved ahead, rather than seek cover behind Vallese. Once again, the elf sorceress set loose a field of sparks. The energy rolled across the ground in front of her, electrical arcs dancing into the enemy. Orcs who couldn't move out of the way were electrocuted on the spot. Two others rushed around the spell, bearing down on the sorceress.

Vallese turned to help Mornik with his opponent. Between the two of them, they made short work of him. Three more approached. Mornik spat, "Behind me, girl. I've lost patience."

Vallese did as he said. The dwarf priest dropped his weapon and shield, focusing both hands in front. He prayed in his own language. As their enemies nearly closed, he thrust out both hands. Vallese didn't see flames, but she felt a blast of heat, even standing behind the dwarf. The air before him distorted, as light wavers when severe heat passes. The orcs stopped in their tracks, throwing up arms to shield themselves. Their hair ignited in flames, skin cracked and darkened. Even the grass between them blackened and smoldered. Three cooked orcs dropped to the ground, followed by Mornik collapsing. Vallese offered him a hand back to his feet.

"Okay, nay more of that until I get some breath back." He said, slightly woozy from the effort. He wobbled as Vallese pulled him upright.

The two remaining orcs facing Cruso and Urgosk turned tail and ran, at least for the moment.

This left all eyes glancing back at the sorceress to witness a transformation. Her hands went from five fingers to four. Fingers and forearms elongated. A moment later, her misshapen hands sported sharp claws. Her arms discolored into a bluish shade, changing into a snake-scale texture. The two orcs who survived Allisee's magic ran within arm's reach, and she caught the arm of the first orc as it descended. Talons digging in, she pulled at him and began to shred the length of his arm. The second orc, overconfident, ignored using his weapon and grabbed her by the throat. Allisee's second deformed arm matched his tactics. Even as he squeezed her throat, she sank her digits into his neck. A wet scream bubbled up as he tried to block her arm. Her companions watched in amazement as Allisee ripped the throat from him. The sorceress turned her attention to the first wounded orc. As it screamed, her claws crossed and re-crossed, ripping sets of X patterns into his torso with every pass. Blood sprayed the elf, once again throwing red stains across the whole of her body. The standing orc fell, the kneeling one tried to rise. One hand covering its damaged throat, it happened to brush an arm against the woman for balance. Allisee reacted instinctively. One claw, then the next, slashed new valleys through his neck. The orc toppled.

The sorceress turned around, her deformed arms seeking to tear apart the next enemy. Red droplets flung from her claws. Her teeth gritted with anger.

She saw the surprised stares of her groupmates. Her expression devolved into horror. Allisee's shame forced her eyes downcast. Her arms melted to their normal shape and size; still bloody, but now trembling. She wanted them to say something, or maybe even forget what they saw.

Volume 1, Chapter 7   "War Wagon"

Mornik took control, "We have to move again. They haven't left us alone."

The others took note of the remaining orcs. A few archers dotted the hills on both sides. A couple started taking shots at the party. Most of the remaining orcs had pulled back. They looked over the numerous corpses and pieces of their tribemates and decided to delay the next attack. Horns continued to blare warnings while drums beat a menacing threat. In the distance, the group could see more forms rushing to join the fight.

"They have endless reinforcements. We have to break free of this engagement," the knight offered.

Urgosk pulled his huge axe from a corpse, "Forge 'head, best way."

They started forward again. Allisee's hesitation to join them was clear. She felt a hand cup her elbow. Vallese stood at her side, a gentle tug urging the elf onward, "Go, we must."

As the group ran, orc archers ran alongside their path, loosing the occasional arrow. Vallese reached for one of hers.

"Don't," the elf said, causing Vallese to pause. "They outnumber your arrows, and they're saving us for something."

Cruso and Urgosk shared her worries, but didn't voice it. Both warriors saw the way their enemies multiplied in the hills, yet onward the group ran down the bramble-barrier trail. The orcs didn't descend for a fight but weren't letting them escape either.

The half-orc grunted, "We've got ta find that mill."

"As good a plan as any," the knight agreed.

Eastward their footsteps charged, closer to the fires and smoke covering those hills. The others began breathing as hard as the dwarf. Sweat began making their armor even more uncomfortable than usual. More orcs joined the chase, running closer to the trail than before. The orcs whooped and hollered, some threw curses.

Urgosk shouted something back, but Allisee admonished him between breaths. "Don't incite them. We want them…more frightened…than angered."

Cruso shouted, "Look ahead! The gaps."

The others followed the knight's pointing finger. Heavier armed orcs stood in lines, shield touching shield. They didn't block the path. The formations closed the sally exits through the bramble gaps.

Vallese cursed, "Trapped on trail!"

"Aye," Mornik added, huffing "Suddenly…I want…new route."

The half-orc pointed out a new threat. At a spot where the trail split, similarly armored orcs blocked other routes to herd the group in a direction of the orcs' choice. The group passed close to one such blockade as they ran. Some of the orcs threw rocks and daggers. One slammed a large, jagged polearm into the ground to intimidate them. The orcs didn't break rank or offer a chase.

"Ha-ra, ha-ra!"

Sir Cruso wiped the sweat from his eyes and glanced at Urgosk, "What causes such mirth?"

"They were wet up to their belts!"

Vallese ran confused, "We made them…wet leggings?"

"The river!" He proclaimed, "It means they crossed the river! Mills sit b'side rivers! It's close!"

The rest couldn't as optimistic as Urgosk. Their lungs and muscles complained as they ran between the endless bramble lines. Orc numbers swelled on both sides. Some called out threats in the local human tongue, Hespal, promising the tortures they would inflict on any they captured. It became a game to the orcs. The five kept running, with no haven in sight. The mass of orcs filled the air with their ruckus.

Vallese's enhanced hearing picked up something new. Something making rhythmic, mechanical noises could be heard approaching from behind. She stole a look back…and felt renewed fear. The archer's pace quickened. She ran past the dwarf and even began to outpace the taller Allisee.

"Run! Run fast!"

The others did what came naturally, they slowed down to look for the cause of concern. The others saw two behemoth wolves growling as they closed the distance. They ran side-by-side, lips curled into snarls and eager drool spraying the ground. Each shared the weight and height of a horse. They pulled an open war wagon behind them. The war wagon stretched from bramble row to bramble row. Spikes and blades spun on the wheels. A scarred driver occupied a center throne on the front. He handled the wolf reins with both hands over a painted, trophy-decorated shield mounted on the front of the cart. Polearm bearers stood on either side of him, behind the protection of the sideboards. Laughter brimmed from their throats and their eyes promised blood as they surged closer. The four wheels of the wagon churned new ruts into the trail as they rolled. Old blood stained the axels.

The Kashmer group shared wide eyes. Before they could break and flee, Mornik bellowed. "Stop here! This is our chance!" The priest glanced over at Urgosk, "Can you drive that?"

The force of his voice brought the rest to a staggering stop. Even Vallese halted, a full fifteen feet beyond the point Urgosk and Cruso hesitated. For a moment, Cruso and Allisee traded glances between the dwarf and the half-orc. Had they misjudged which one was the craziest of them?

Urgosk replied, "I can, if it doesn't mash me!"

As the large chariot thundered closer, Allisee shook her head. "He's right. This will kill us or be our ticket to freedom. But how?"

Vallese set her feet and notched an arrow. "Right polearm."

Urgosk hefted a javelin, "Left polearm."

Allisee called, "I've got the driver," even though she could barely see his eyes over the wagon-mounted shield protecting him.

Mornik stood next to Allisee, "We'll time our spells to throw fear into those mongrels."

Orcs on the hills stopped and cheered as they saw the adventurers stop in the path of their machine. The driver laughed even more obnoxiously than Urgosk as he urged his beasts onward. Slobber ran from the mouths of the huge wolves as they anticipated a snack.

Sir Cruso felt less useful than the others in stopping the wagon. A thought came to him. "How are you boarding it?"

"Dunno." Urgosk shrugged.

"Nay idea." Allisee stared at the crushing wheels.

Mornik tried to sound hopeful, "My trick might slow it."

The knight came to a decision. "Follow me, I'll be your ramp." He moved several steps ahead of the others, careful to not get in anyone's aim.

Time ran short. Mornik began a countdown. Vallese's bowstring stretched taut. Orcs nearly drowned out everything by their excited voices, everything except the rambling of the bladed wheels over the trail. Sir Cruso tried to concentrate on what he needed to do, while trying not to think about how much it would likely hurt. He set sword in scabbard and only left his shield in his hands.

Mornik's countdown ended. Vallese's arrow flew away for the strike. The laughter of one polearm-bearer stopped as the arrow penetrated the leather covering its neck. The weapon dropped as its hands flew up defensively.

Urgosk's javelin launched into the air. The other armed orc barely saw it coming before Mornik's miracle blinded them. The dwarf priest created an explosion of flames stretching across the trail. The orc forgot about the javelin until it punched into his gut.

The flames panicked the wolves. The driver fought the reins as the beasts tried to flee in opposite directions. Their paws skidded the ground, claws digging ruts, as they tried to stop. Hitched as they were, the momentum of the wagon dragged them forward as a surge of electricity blinded them momentarily. The reins went slack as charred bits of the driver fell over the melting shield.

The wolves stumbled through the flames…flames that didn't even burn. Mornik's illusion gave off some heat, but lacked the capacity to burn anything. Sir Cruso met the wagon head-on. He tossed his shield into the air, hoping it would land in the wagon. The beasts' eyes hadn't cleared and the knight jumped between them, arms spread wide. Cruso's arms closed on the leather harnesses, while his legs and body fell over the neck yolks and the wagon tongue. The knight scrambled for balance on the long beam. His weight threw the point of the tongue into the dirt. Luckily, it had been designed with a slight curve, sliding across the dirt rather than digging in. Cruso's body also pulled the wolves' heads toward the ground.

Mornik eyed the wagon tongue, smothered by Cruso, as it slid toward him. The knight was using his sprawled body as a ramp up into the wagon. The wagon slowed as its weighted tongue skidded along the path, but it still approached as fast as a human could run. Mornik stalled as he realized there was no way he could climb the knight's back and run up to the driver's seat.

Urgosk shouted, "Dwarf toss!"

Mornik's mouth barely opened wide in surprise as he felt strong hands grab him. A bounce and a glance over the shoulder revealed Urgosk's red irises. The half-orc's willpower surged with his berserker rage. Mornik stuttered in anger as he felt his feet leave the ground. Two steps propelled the half-orc before the priest went flying.

Urgosk continued his run, landing a foot on Cruso's back. The knight felt the air blast from his lungs even as dust and pebbles assaulted his face. The half-orc kept running, heedless of Cruso's difficulties keeping a handhold. Urgosk's second step managed to land higher on the bouncing tongue. The berserker flung himself forward with all his rage, jumping toward the driver's seat.

Allisee bolted for the path of the wagon once her lightning spell launched at the driver. Starting behind Mornik and Urgosk, she thought the way would be bottle-necked as they all ran for the same spot. As it was, the nimble elf caught up to Urgosk directly over Cruso. The knight didn't get a chance at air as the slender sorceress also ran up his back. Allisee collided with Urgosk's back, then began to fall forward. Without thinking, her hands flailed and latched onto his belt. Urgosk's jump yanked her along.

Vallese also caught up to the others as they were using poor Cruso as a springboard, but she knew without a doubt she couldn't follow the crowd before the rolling wagon threatened her. The affinity of the panther ran through her blood as she charged between a wolf and the bordering brambles. She threw her bow like a spear up to the wagon. The crushing, spiked wheels bore directly towards her. Her hands caught the wolf's harness. With a foreign cry, she put all her effort into swinging her feet, followed by the rest of her body, into the air. Senses spinning as she tumbled through the air, she could only hope her aim proved true.

In quick succession, a number of things landed inside the wagon bed. Two dying orcs thrashed as they fell. The remaining bottom half of the driver slumped down. A green-and-yellow patterned shield bounced off one orc before settling. A cursing priest dropped from the heavens. Heel fell, led by its backspike, sending splinters from the floorboard. A berserk half-orc soared in, slamming chunks out of the damaged driver's seat. A flailing elf woman followed the half-orc, landing on top of him. The bow made from unknown wood bounced off Mornik's neck, drawing more curses. A dark-skinned human rolled over all the bodies, gashing her skin on the red-gold plates of a shield dedicated to Nandorrin. Before anything or anyone came to rest, the tongue of the wagon impacted a rut in the trail. After the wagon gave a sudden hop, people and equipment landed in a different arrangement. The large wolves yelped at the tug on their harnesses, continuing at a walk.

Urgosk found himself more or less where he wanted to be: in the driver's seat, though Allisee's slender kicking legs obstructed his view when she landed. Grunting, he grabbed an ankle and thrust it aside, sending Allisee tumbling into the wagon bed. The half-orc immediately grabbed at the reins while looking for Cruso, who had disappeared from the wagon tongue.

"Paladin! Where ya at?"

Disheveled Mornik, fearing the worst, looked behind the wagon. "Nandorrin's Beard! He's being dragged!"

Urgosk craned his neck to see. "He went *under* the wagon?"

The dwarf was too busy to respond. A length of leather from the harnesses up front tangled around one arm, caught in a joint of the armor. Cruso spat blood and dirt as he bounced behind the wagon. Mornik got his hands on Cruso's free arm.

Straining, the dwarf shouted, "I need help!"

Vallese slipped a pair of fingers into one of her pouches. Feeling the familiar bone claw, she mouthed. *Bear spirit, give me strength.* The woman braced herself against the low backboard of the wagon. Her tattooed arms joined the dwarf's as they struggled with the knight's weight. She paid no mind to the injuries she received when landing on Mornik's shield. Blood drops trickled down the scratches on her back.

The dwarf growled, "Urgosk! Slow down and give us a…forget it! Go, go!"

A bounce of the knight and a tug from both helpers got Cruso's free arm over the backboard. Arrows began to whistle in from the hills of angry orcs. Allisee barely regained her feet only to be struck by one. The arrow embedded in the side of her pelvis. She surrendered an anguished cry before falling against the back of the driver's seat.

Urgosk struggled with the large wolves. They weren't happy about the new scents behind them. One wolf snapped its head back trying to take a bite out of the new driver. When it tried for a second bite, Urgosk's fist bloodied its lip.

"Ok bakra! Ok bakra!"

The wolves, cowed by his fist and voice, picked up speed.

Archer and priest counted and heaved as one. Cruso helped as best he could. Blood ran down one side of his face. Bit by bit, they managed to get him draped over the backboard. Vallese struggled with the harness, until she noticed Cruso's parrying dagger in its back sheath. The woman drew it and managed to saw her way through the harness. Once freed, the two companions dragged the battered knight into the wagon bed. Cruso could only groan as all three collapsed from the strain of their efforts.

Knocks and thunks echoed against the wagon sides. The orc archers proved vengeful about being deprived of their sport and their war chariot. Waves of arrows launched after the speeding vehicle. A razor-sharp point pierced one of Urgosk's arms. The half-orc howled in pain. His curses at the wolves doubled.

Allisee still had a spell that could help. She began to bring it to the forefront of her mind, struggling against the pain in her hip. Her concentration scattered a moment later as one of the dying orcs in the wagon proved he still had fight in him. The orc's arm came out of the pile of equipment and drove a dagger blade into her leg.

The sorceress' anger flared. A new spell jumped to the front of her mind, and she let it flow. Her finger jabbed the arm and sank an overwhelming electrical charge into it. The appendage swelled and a seam burst open. Allisee knew with sickening certainty that, underneath the equipment, the rest of the orc looked the same. She almost succumbed to the pain, but her will stubbornly held. Allisee's eyes sought help from her groupmates.

Still shielded from arrows by the protection of the sideboards, Mornik's healing hands tried to fix the damage Cruso suffered.

Vallese met Allisee's eyes and seemed to share the elf's sense of desperation. The archer knew better than to sit and wait for help. The gashes from her landing still dripped blood. Vallese produced a healing potion and drank. She looked at the scores of orcs in the area and knew her quiver didn't hold enough arrows.

Allisee cocked her head to the side, listening to Urgosk's strained breathing. "Ok bakra! Gobda, muwata. Ok bakra!"

His words wheezed from his lungs. Allisee could see blood dripping down the side of the seat. An arrow sailed over the sideboard and bounced off Heel.

They need this spell. She drew a shuddering breath. *I can't fail them.*

The sorceress called upon the wind. Every bounce of the wagon jarred her wounds and threatened her concentration. She tried to elevate her spirit beyond her body. Her essence mixed with the air currents. Wind forces began howling around the wagon. Orc arrows continued to rain, but Allisee's storm tossed them aside. The torrential wind guardian stripped leaves and berries from the brambles as they passed. Their opponents could see the privateers clearly, but couldn't hit their targets. The wolf-pulled wagon thundered between hills of orcs, a torrent of air keeping it safe.

Urgosk felt his body begin to tip forward. His head jerked up, digging into his dwindling reserves of anger to keep conscious. A lithe body slipped in beside his perch. A dark hand slapped at his chest.

"You save me!" Vallese's words were a command. "You brought me, now get me out! Drink healing potion!"

In order to heal him, she first yanked the arrow from his body. That brought a moment of crystal clarity to his senses, as well as a roar from his throat. Urgosk almost laughed at a secret joke as her hands uncorked the flask hanging from his neck. She shoved the opening to his lips, and he eagerly obliged. The liquid burned down to his gut. He welcomed the taste.

The woman lowered the bottle. To her surprise, the arrow wound still bled.

"Nuttin' magic 'bout this stuff, darlin'. Just alcohol."

The half-orc kept smiling as he slid out of the seat and tumbled down unconscious by the elf. Vallese managed to grab the reins, but she stood frozen. How could she drive this thing? Her attachment to animal spirits revealed one dangerous aspect…the wolves sensed weakness and began slowing.

The sorceress had an answer, but the spell protecting the wagon enslaved her voice. How could she get a message to the other woman? Allisee despised the only solution…to surrender a little bit of herself into the monster within her. Her hands shifted into claws. Vallese proved too busy to hear the scratching on the side of the driver's seat. The elf urgently tapped her talons against the wood. Finally, the archer looked down at the elf's malformed hands…and the message carved into the wood.

OK BAKRA

Vallese recalled Urgosk shouting the words. The archer jumped into the driver's seat and snapped the reins, yelling the strange words over and over. Her affinity for animal spirits suddenly gave her an edge. She understood, better than the half-orc, how the wolves liked to move and the path they tried to pick. The wagon surged forward, racing past the lines of orcs. Several enemies attempted pursuit, but they had no mounts. The numbers of orcs thinned as the group raced along.

Allisee reached for a potion at her belt. As expensive as jewelry, healing potions were priceless in times like this. She pulled it free and prepared to flick the cork with her thumb. She craved a drink to remedy her pain. Regrettably, the wounds wouldn't heal unless the arrow and dagger were pulled from her body, but doing so would break her spell. The wind element continued to swirl around the wagon, tossing aside arrows, saving their lives. At least she could assist someone else. The sorceress flicked the cork and forced the opening into Urgosk's smelly mouth. Allisee didn't have to worry about choking him. The divinity of the potion would heal him regardless of entry into his system. The elf put faith that Mornik's healing would reach her in time.

Cruso's wounds were extensive. As Mornik channeled divine aid, the knight's breathing evened out and he began to move his limbs. The dwarf, confidant in Cruso's recovery, drew in a deep breath and looked around. His eyes quickly took in their dire situation.

"Some really experienced priests can heal an entire group of friends in close proximity to them. Sadly, you only have me. I'll do my best." The chosen of Nandorrin moved from person to person, channeling the divinity of his god into them. His healing spells felt like a fire swarming into their wounds.

Only Allisee waved him off. She pointed at her wounds, then at her spellcasting mouth, and the dwarf understood her concern. The elf endured her suffering as he moved to everyone else. Urgosk regained consciousness and vigor, and Vallese's wounds healed, but Mornik nearly passed out from exertion.

Noticing that Mornik seemed ready to swoon, Urgosk shifted closer to him. The half-orc splashed the strong alcohol in his flask into the dwarf's face and mouth. Mornik sputtered at the strong taste. It worked wonders to open his eyes.

"We'll be limited to potions until I can recover," said Mornik as he pulled several flasks from his bags. "I don't have the strength to channel more healing right now."

Urgosk was in awe, "That cost a small fortune. Or did ya make 'em?"

"Someday I plan to craft these, but I'm not quite good enough yet. These are all I have left from my homeland; a gift when I left on my pilgrimage." Mornik's beard twisted with his smirk, "Even in my dreams it feels as if I've walked continents."

The potions worked miracles for the rest. Mornik faced Allisee. "We've outrun most of the orcs. It's time we get you healed."

She dropped her incantations. "I'm ready."

Her eyes seemed to tell a different story as Urgosk put a hand on both the arrow and the dagger. He yanked them out before she could protest. Her screams ended as Mornik shoved a healing potion to her mouth and forced her to drink.

*

Urgosk guided the war wagon with Vallese at his side as they thundered closer to the plumes of black smoke. The half-orc exclaimed, "I think I see the mill!"

The wagon rounded a hill and view before them opened up, bringing anxiety as well as their goal. They clearly saw a large, stone building outlined against a valley of smoke. On the far side, a giant wheel turned along with the current.

Sir Cruso agreed, "Mill is there, other side of the river."

The elf hissed as she sucked air between her teeth. "They've got a barricade blocking the bridge."

Mornik gestured to the noise from the surrounding hills. "We couldn't outrace the drum signals."

"Turn!" Vallese poked the half-orc.

"Where?"

The trail followed a runoff of stream water between two hills. Their course aimed straight down to the bridge, with no room to turn easily. The road forked near the bridge, running along both directions along the river. There was little time to argue a solution. Orcs on the bridge could be seen raising their bows. Piles of crates and sacks, likely from the mill, blocked the crossing.

"One indisputable thing I can tell you," the priest sounded anxious, "I'm almost out of healing ability. The less fighting, the better."

Urgosk noticed Allisee staring at him. "What?"

"You want to get into that mill, don't you? Find the way down below?"

"Argh, I've become predictable!"

Cruso shook his head, "Predictably crazy! Too risky to fight past the bridge into the mill…"

The elf pointed to the right of the bridge, an almost direct line to the mill. "We have to turn now, go directly for it." She turned toward the dwarf. "You have energy for some false flames, I hope?"

"Aye, but…wait. You can't be serious!"

Urgosk guided the war wagon into a slight turn. They aimed directly for the mill, despite the river in the way. Their direct path took them uphill, towards a ridge overhanging the river. The wolves leading the wagon couldn't see the river beyond the ridge.

Cruso looked at their course with wide eyes. "Can everyone stop taking turns coming up with *crazy* plans?"

"When we're close..." she started, but never finished. Instead, Allisee began whistling an incantation. The others saw wind kick up around the wagon. Just in time, her windstorm deflected a hail of arrows launched from the bridge.

"I git the idea," Urgosk winked at her. He glanced at Mornik. "Git yer fake flames ready to dance on the harnesses."

"Nay!"

"I ain't stoppin'!"

Everyone began to hold on tight to the wagon as the intent became apparent. The wagon raced up the ridge, straight at the cliff overhanging the river. The dwarf pulled out a waterproof bladder, squeezing the holy water out of it. The bridge remained a long bowshot upriver from the group. Mornik began to blow air into the now-empty holy water bladder, filling it like a balloon. Orcs on the bridge continued to fire arrows and curse. The arrows which came close couldn't get through the elf's barrier. Mornik began a prayer as they approached the cliff. Illusionary flames spread upon the wolves' harnesses and the wagon tongue. The wolves, panicking, broke into a fearful run.

"Let's see how she flies!" Urgosk cheered. "First Hand!"

The wagon didn't fly well at all, quickly nosing down the moment it zoomed off the cliff's edge, despite the wolves trying to jump away from the false flames. The group felt as if their stomachs were rising into their throats. Next to the mill, the river ran narrow but deep. They realized the wagon would land close to the middle, with about forty feet separating them from the far side. Mornik and Sir Cruso barely got their hands on their shields before deciding to abandon the wagon. The wolves hit the water with a resounding splash. The wagon splintered and buckled in places as it hit. Five forms dove into the water next to it.

Vallese hit the water like a natural swimmer. Less encumbered than most of her party, she easily kicked her way to the shallows on the opposite side. As her torso broke above the water, she spotted a couple orc guards rushing out of cover near the mill. She hurried a few quick steps and whipped her bow off her shoulder. Her other arm reached for an arrow. Empty quiver. Her remaining arrows drifted away after the fall!

She threw the bow at the closest orc, buying time to unshoulder her staff instead. Vallese barely got her weapon in-line to deflect its axe. The second orc closed in as well. She fought defensively as both enemies tried to surround her. Trapped as she was against the river, they had the advantage.

Allisee's thin blade snaked in from Vallese's right, leaving a line of red across an orc's arm. That opponent backed off, its momentum shifted to a defensive posture as the elf blade twitched and stabbed. Allisee gave her friend time to recover. The archer felt it a bad sign that the sorceress resorted to her weapon instead of her talents.

The orc with the axe almost lost his weapon as Vallese spun her staff. He proved patient for an orc. He wasn't allowing for mistakes, despite Vallese managing to push him away from the river's edge.

His concentration broke when the other battle reached an unexpected conclusion. Allisee and her opponent sparred without a victor…until a two-handed axe carried by a wet half-orc joined the fight. The orc went down in halves. As the remaining orc spared a glance, Vallese hooked her staff under the axe blade and twisted it from his grip. She followed with a swing that cracked across the orc's neck.

"The others?" Allisee faced the river, only to watch the wagon and its team of wolves bobbing downstream. A glance at it revealed how valuable the sorceress' wind shield had been. Dozens of orc arrow shafts protruded from the wagon bed. The giant wolves howled and yipped as the current pulled them with the sinking wagon.

"Thought I saw Paladin's helm stickin' 'bove the water…"

No sooner than Urgosk said it, they saw Cruso's forearm thrust out of the water, holding his helm. A moment later, it disappeared back under the water. Urgosk and Vallese dropped their weapons and waded back into the river. Going the opposite way, Allisee had to circle the mill to view upstream.

The orcs from the bridge were approaching. She decided to deter them. The sorceress fired an electric bolt across the distance. One unlucky orc dropped from spasms. The rest took cover, rethinking their strategy. Allisee hoped they didn't see her go weak in the knees from the effort. The more magic she cast without rest, the harder it would be to keep forming spells.

Voices in the river grabbed her attention.

"Ya drank air out of yer helmet? Ha-ra, ha-ra!"

Cruso spoke between gasps. "Well, I could only walk along the bottom. Is everyone fair?"

"Nay dwarf yet. Heavyboot doesn't float."

"There!" Vallese pointed, "Bubbles from something!"

Vallese helped Cruso stagger the final steps onto shore as Urgosk ran to the source of the bubbles. The half-orc dove under the churning current. Mornik's body broke the surface, hoisted upon muscular shoulders. The priest's former holy water bladder, still slightly inflated, was in his mouth. He pulled it out. The dwarf sucked a fresh breath as the leather bag deflated. His face began to lose its blue hue.

"I shouldn't have to tell you all," He gasped. "Your priest is your healing. My life is your life. Don't get your priest killed."

Allisee glanced upriver. The orcs began reforming their ranks. This time, they were linking a shield wall together.

The elf turned everyone's attention to the problem. "We still need to find that underground entry. I have little strength left for spells. Vallese lacks arrows. Do we have anything with range that can slow their advance?"

Urgosk noted with dismay that he, too, had lost his javelins. Sir Cruso checked his belt.

"My folding crossbow may still work. The bolts are sealed in this pouch." The knight confirmed they were present. "Check the mill, I will slow them."

"Hand me a bolt," the dwarf said once his feet hit solid ground. "I have a trick I can use."

Urgosk led the charge into the mill, followed closely by Vallese and Allisee. Sir Cruso and Mornik ducked into cover at the corner of the building. Cruso assembled his crossbow in record time. The knight felt relief that he couldn't hear any sounds of fighting inside the mill as he hurried. Pins and gears held the arms in position as he dropped a bolt into the firing groove. He aimed at the approaching shield line of orcs. The weapon jerked slightly as it fired, but the bolt broke harmlessly against a shield.

As Cruso spun a crank that pulled back the strings, the orcs hurried forward. Mornik handed him the borrowed bolt. "Send that in, but give me a countdown before you fire."

The bolt had a wad of cloth stuck on the end. Some oil on the cloth fed a small flame. As the human warrior took aim, the orcs quickly jammed their shields together again.

Mornik began a prayer as Cruso counted, "3…2…1…"

The priest's prayer ended with 'Rutan' as the bolt launched. The flames licking the cloth increased a hundredfold. The orcs screamed and broke ranks as a fireball flew toward them. Several tumbled out of the way as their screams of terror carried to the mill. The bolt incinerated itself before it reached the target, leaving a wave of heat passing through their numbers.

"That had more bark than bite," Sir Cruso laughed, "But it left quite a scare."

Mornik plucked another bolt from Cruso's case. "If you don't mind…"

*

Urgosk ran into the mill swinging his axe. He managed to nick a support beam, eviscerate a bag of seeds, and disembowel a sack of fruit, but found no enemies present. The gears of the mill went on grinding away unattended. Vallese and Allisee flanked him as they found safe room to do so. Allisee pointed her thin sword at every corner, the Vallese kept her staff cocked for a swing.

"There! They left it open!" Allisee declared.

A rug had been pulled aside and a hidden floorboard hatch stood propped-open. A sloped tunnel with reinforced sides that looked slightly wet descended away from the river. Urgosk approached the hatch and took the first step down.

"The others?" Vallese asked.

Urgosk held up a hand, "Let 'em delay a bit. Need to see if it's safe."

The half-orc descended into the darkness, his eyes allowing him to see well. Allisee followed a few footsteps behind. Urgosk followed the tunnel into an antechamber and through two turns. He stopped before a lever in the wall.

"What's this?" The barbarian checked out a mechanism disappearing into the wall. He glanced back to the ceiling over Allisee's head. "We've found our escape!"

The sorceress narrowed her eyes at the lever, "What's that do?"

"Saves us," was the only reply. "Get the others!"

Allisee ran back outside and yelled for Mornik and Cruso. The priest and the knight had been using the corner of the building and a stack of goods for cover. The call came just as the orcs were almost upon the mill.

"Go on," urged the priest, "I'll slow them up."

As Sir Cruso hoisted his crossbow and ran over to the door, Mornik let loose another spell. A field of warm flames spread between the mill and the nearby hillside. In frustration, the orcs threw spears or fired bows at the retreating dwarf, but they couldn't see him through the fire. If any had dared chance it, they would have found the flames to be another illusion. The rest of the Kashmer group raced down the tunnel.

"All of ya, git behind me!" Urgosk directed. He caught Cruso's eyes as the knight caught up. Urgosk pointed further down the passage. "Paladin, see what's down there."

Sir Cruso led the way down the next tunnel. The rest spread out between the two warriors, unsure whether to stick with the knight or see what the half-orc had planned. Cruso felt severely disadvantaged while scouting. The orcs had a light system in place, consisting of baskets of glowing plants and illuminated symbols, the latter of which sent shivers down his spine as he couldn't be sure they weren't a trap. Neither light source offered sufficient illumination for Cruso to feel comfortable moving fast. Vallese joined him. He was grateful to have someone close who, by whatever means, seemed able to see in the dark a lot better than he could. Cruso and Vallese discovered numerous passages branching away. They weren't gone long before returning within sight of Urgosk to report their findings.

The knight offered, "A larger chamber, then the tunnels start branching different ways. Looks like we've entered a large cave system."

"Good, I'd hoped we weren't trapped. Stand back! I hear 'em comin'." Urgosk spit on his hands before gripping the lever. Vallese and Allisee tucked back near Cruso as they heard orc shouts echoing out in the mill.

The dwarf, after stopping to examine the tunnel leading to the lever, sensed the weakness in the walls. "You sure about what you're planning?" He asked.

Urgosk grinned, "Guessin' plenty of ways out, but this sounds like the only one they left to git in."

Ferocious orcs screamed as they rounded the far corner. Jagged weapons promised blood. The orcs saw Urgosk at the lever, and the pitch of their screams changed. The lead ones tried to sprint faster, if only to stop the half-orc in time.

Urgosk pulled the lever. Somewhere to the side, a counterweight dropped. It ripped away supports holding up the ceiling, causing rocks and earth to drop on the charging orcs. The tunnel rumbled and shook. Even walls behind the companions cracked as a result.

The lead orc managed to stay just ahead of the deadfall, until a swing from Mornik's Heel sent him reeling back into it. The entry filled floor-to-ceiling with rocks and choking dust. The rumble settled, leaving the hall blocked. Urgosk and Mornik turned from the rubble and rejoined the others.

Allisee stood in the dim light, blocking the tunnel, glaring at the half-orc through her vertical pupils. "You do a lot of planning one step at a time, don't you?"

The roguish half-orc helplessly held his hands out wide, shrugged, and grinned.

Volume 1, Chapter 8   **Bowels of the Orc Fortress**

"Anyone remember the name?" Vallese asked.

They were resting in a large room as Urgosk performed another scouting run. They felt less secure here than in other places. After the commotion at the secret door, the group ventured a short way into the tunnels before being led into a spot that veered off the main tunnels. Urgosk had already redirected several orcs that came to investigate the noise. It bought them time. The companions feared it wouldn't take long for enough orcs to swarm the area and discover them.

Cruso took his eyes off the passage he was guarding. A flickering light from his shield, bestowed by Mornik, illuminated the room's exit. "I'm sorry, what name?"

"The noble."

Allisee withdrew a slip of paper from a pocket. "Lord Felnick Pentle, nephew to the Lord Mayor of Kashmer, and a few spots down in line for a throne." She folded it and returned it to her pocket.

A snore nearly drowned out her words, and all three turned their eyes to Mornik. The dwarf slumped on a hide couch, legs splayed out, a line of drool on his beard.

The elf observed, "He's overplayed his miracles."

Sir Cruso didn't miss the way the elf leaned against the wall. It practically held up her weight. He said, "We are all in need of a rest, but those orcs will deny us the chance. Best to push on until we find a way out." The knight threw a worried look down the passageway. Hearing nothing, he took a moment to stretch his arms and shoulders. Cruso looked back to Vallese and Allisee once again. "Stay behind me, I was born and raised to shield those I care about."

She returned his gaze. "Lord's son? Trained from a young age with wooden swords?"

He nodded and grinned as he recalled a fond memory. She continued, "Do they really train several horses, or just pick one?"

A weary smile emerged from within his once well-groomed mustache and beard, now sullied by their rough road. "Takes a long time to train a horse. You split your time between several, but eventually, you find a favorite. Still, different horses may excel better at one tournament or another. It's good to keep a large stable."

Allisee tried to imagine the knight's history. The elf glanced at Vallese, who paced back and forth near the dwarf. The woman's eyes kept darting to the entrance, as if expecting trouble at any moment. Her obvious anxiety denied her a proper rest.

Allisee asked Cruso, "What different kinds of tournaments do they have?"

"There is the martial kind, of course. Guiding your steed with just your legs while you joust, trying to knock the other from his saddle. You can also compete spearing rings at a full gallop. I have enjoyed watching many sword-and-shield competitions between teams of riders. Other games display excellent prowess between horse and rider without weapons involved. There are races and jump courses; you may also perform specific movements and steps called dressage for prizes. Well, sometimes simply prestige."

"And you champion someone? Doesn't your title bind you to a higher lord in times of war?"

Allisee didn't miss how the smile suddenly disappeared. Cruso's gaze drifted downward, happiness replaced by something unpleasant. She thought she would hit a nerve with that question, and the human proved her right.

Before any more could be said, a deep thud sounded somewhere distant. The floor trembled for the briefest of moments. Motes of dirt and dust shook from the support rafters.

Cruso raised his shield, despite the lack of any immediate threat. "Great Dalios, what strength was that?" The knight held his divinely-lit shield before the open door, illuminating the hallway.

Urgosk appeared a moment later, running back to them. "Time ta git our prize!"

Allisee beseeched him, "What did you do?"

The half-orc shrugged, "T'wasn't me! But the native orcs are up there, gathered fer a last stand. The Kashmer Army is somewhere just above. I'm guessin' things are about ta collide. We best find the hole they planted this prince and spring 'im."

The sorceress pulled the wand from her belt. She said a single word and she tapped it to her side: she could feel the magical protection cover her once again. The elf felt a wave of relief. She wasn't sure how much more the wand could deliver without recharging it.

Vallese was already jostling the dwarf. "Wake up! On feet!"

"I'm awake! I've been contemplating the relationship between Nandorrin and the other element gods!"

"Awake? You rumble, make honk-snuff noise, could wake dead!"

Mornik scoffed as he rose to his feet. "That must be someone else. I don't snore."

The ground shook again, more rumbles echoing from a distance. This wasn't just one tremor, but a slew of relentless vibrations. Foreign curses from just down the hall spooked the party, and Sir Cruso saw them first. Figures moved at the edge of his light. One turned his way. He could see the shield's firelight reflected in its eyes.

"Codex guide me!"

The knight's legs pounded the tunnel floor, shoving aside his half-orc partner. The orcs in the hall drew weapons as he closed. Urgosk fell into step behind Cruso. The rest ran out of the room in pursuit.

The human bore only his shield as he ran. The orcs tried to line up a stab, but Cruso held the shield across his body, helm bobbing above the rim. The orcs could easily make out the heraldry: white horse, on the yellow and green diamond field. The dwarf flames blazing from shield commanded attention. Mesmerizing and protective, it slammed into the first orc while the enemy still tried to figure how to attack. Cruso's legs relentlessly pounded forward. The first orc fell under the shield, and still Cruso pushed ahead. His armored boots trampled the orc as the second one felt the force of the shield's slam.

The first orc had no time to recover. As soon as the trampling boots clambered over it, it opened its eyes and saw the descending axe. Urgosk yanked the edge free of the corpse with one hand, using the other to push Cruso onward.

"That's the spirit, Paladin!"

The second orc fell under the shield and boots as well. It managed to wrap Cruso's leg, only briefly, before a heavy axe separated the orc from the world of the living.

They stumbled into a cross tunnel, shouts coming from both directions. "Right!" Urgosk urged. Once again, he planted a hand on Cruso's back to help keep his momentum and shift him in the correct direction.

Following everyone, Vallese could see something that the others tried to conceal. The knight's tactics sacrificed skillful swordplay. He leaned into his shield and tried to follow with his legs. The orcs overrun by his shield inadvertently pushed it, maintaining the warrior's balance. As Urgosk pushed Cruso from behind, he also served to keep himself upright. Urgosk spared one hand on his large axe. As he moved over the trampled orcs, he didn't hit them with the axe so much as he let it drop. The weight of the weapon managed to finish its portion of the work. It occurred to the archer that the half-orc had to be the most exhausted of them all. Every time they stopped to hide and catch a breath, Urgosk was always out scouting. As Cruso took a sharp turn down a new hall, momentum carried Urgosk into the wall. The half-orc bounced off, using the collision to realign his course.

The sorceress abandoned any use of magic or her terrifying claws in favor of her thin blade. Allisee stabbed the downed orcs with her sword as she passed. Vallese noted the tip sometimes dinged against the underlying floor, flexing as though a walking stick to help push the sorceress further along. The elf's legs did not move as nimbly as before.

The priest's actions proved the biggest revelation. He wheezed and huffed as he stepped along. Earlier, he had given any fallen orcs a 'parting shot' that guaranteed a ticket to their pagan paradise. Now, he simply raised and dropped Heel on them as he went around them.

Positioned in the back, Vallese saw the exhaustion in her peers, and she couldn't deny the weariness in her own body. Her connection to animal spirits bolstered her muscles, driving her beyond what most humans could accomplish. Those same muscles had endured much; every step brought tightness and risked injury. Her will to continue would have faltered if not for the pressing dangers around them, and fear strengthened her stride. Vallese knew they would find no relief in this forsaken hole, but for the moment they broke free of enemies.

The half-orc stooped to pull a hatchet from a downed orc's grip. "Down that passage, it runs 'long the main tunnel!" Urgosk directed.

Sir Cruso altered their course, aiming for an opening on the far side of a branching chamber. The knight settled his shield in place on his left arm. His right drew his steel sword. A few surprised orcs strolled about the chamber. Most didn't have the look of warriors. Female orcs and their children milled about carts filled with mushrooms; nooks in the stone walls held assortments of fruits, dried meat hung from lines, and covered clay jars sat in rows. A male wearing thin garb and wielding metal tongs stepped into their path. Cruso threatened him with upraised sword. Surprising the orc, he delivered a shield bash instead and sent the orc merchant tumbling over a box. As the back of the group passed the downed merchant, only Vallese gave it a second blow. She rapped her staff upon its knee. The human hoped it would deter any more heroics from that one. As the group ran through the undercity's market, most orcs got out of the way.

An armed guard appeared ahead. Urgosk let fly the hatchet he'd yanked from the last enemy. It ripped into the orc's weapon arm.

Vallese spotted a new threat to the side. "Archers!"

Sir Cruso reached the tunnel. A flick of his sword further wounded the guard's weapon hand. The orc dropped his axe and voiced pain. Urgosk pulled the hatchet from the screaming orc's wound without slowing his run.

Allisee reacted to Vallese's warning. Passing a stack of plates on a cart, she reached out and grabbed the top three. The elf tossed them at the approaching danger. Arrows shot wildly as the incoming plates fouled their owners' aim.

As the party ran into the narrower tunnel, Vallese pulled one final act to thwart any pursuers. She grabbed the top of a cart as she passed, yanking it down, and then followed the rest into the passage as the cart and its contents spilled onto the floor. The first orcs to jump the obstruction in pursuit slipped on round fruits. Other orcs tripped over the first ones.

The group ran down a tunnel lit by a mix of glowing marks and divine receptacles. While still rather dim, the light miracle placed upon Cruso's shield by Mornik allowed him to see well enough to lead. He sidestepped containers, ducked low supports, and kept his sword ready in case any of the several side doors opened as they ran. Pursuers echoed behind them.

A door slammed ahead, but Sir Cruso didn't see a threat. As they came upon the door, they spotted a dropped candle and some paper scrolls on the floor. There was no sign of the owner. Mornik saw the items and called out.

"Vallese, help me."

The dwarf grabbed a few nearby items that cluttered the hall: a discarded shawl, a bundle of sticks destined to be future arrow shafts, a broken pole, the scrolls and a wooden crate. With Vallese's help, he made a quick pile around the lit candle.

Mornik spoke, "That will do, let's be off!"

They ran to catch the others. After a few steps, the dwarf glanced back at the candle and prayed, "…Rutan!"

The sputtering flame from the dropped candle ignited into a blaze. The items caught fire, quickly growing to a size that would block pursuit.

*

They stumbled through the network of corridors. Urgosk tried to direct them by intuition, but occasionally orc resistance made the choice for them. They were almost swarmed by pursuers at one point. After locking a door into place, Cruso laid out a false trail at one other exit. The group slid down a smelly chute, landing in a room full of waste. Piles of discarded food and everyday items lie at the base of other chutes. A rancid stream of sewage flowed through, and all were relieved they avoided it upon landing. They laid aside their revulsion in favor of survival. In no time the group resumed a run. There were few enough orcs moving about this level that Urgosk took the lead as scout.

When they had a chance to duck into a closed chamber, Urgosk once again ran ahead. Vallese had only ever felt this tired one other time in her life. She wasn't sure how she survived then, and didn't know how she would live out this escapade. Her companions looked just as exhausted. Allisee succumbed to a hide-backed chair, her eyes dropping closed. Mornik, out of spite for their hosts, selected someone's food table and sat on it while trying to wipe clean the waste from his clothes. Sir

Cruso stood just inside the door, but his weight leaned into the wall. Vallese eased her breathing. None of the others spared breath for words.

Urgosk returned minutes later, "He's close. Didn't see 'im, but they're rallyin' this way. Somehow, Kashmer punched into the tunnels. I know which way to go."

Everyone bravely stood without complaint, though they moved forward with slumped shoulders and dragging feet. Vallese wished for something she could do to assist them, but Allisee spoke the words that rallied them.

"We can do this. We've run a crazy road these last few days, but we're here. You've all proven strong. Now we need to call on our reserve strength." She took the time to look each in the eyes as she spoke their names. "Urgosk. Sir Cruso. Mornik. Vallese. I've been blessed to be in this team. Our goal is just around a corner or two. Tell me you have a little more left in you, and I swear to you we will make it through."

The others visibly straightened at her words. Sir Cruso rolled his shoulders, readjusting his glowing shield. He stood every bit his 6' 2" frame and more. The knight mouthed the words of a prayer he uttered whenever they stopped long enough for him to read from his small Codex. Allisee watched and understood his words: "Dalios grant me strength of arm, Ganden forge me the shield of honor, and *The Codex* guide me on the righteous path."

Mornik brushed a hand through his unruly hair. His fingers forced their way through the brownish-red snarls. "This small-clan has a lot of fire." He fished the chain with his holy symbol out of his beard. The dim light reflected in the twin hammers crossed over a forge. "These halls *will* be scorched with our cleansing flames."

Urgosk already wore a crazy grin in the midst of his bloody warpaint. One jagged fingernail picked at his yellow teeth. Though Allisee had already considered his hair greasy and unkempt, the last few days made it even more repugnant. He saw her eyes upon him and shrugged, "I'm First Hand! Enemies feed my rage when they hurt me."

Vallese stretched. A few of her joints popped and cracked as they moved in ways most humans couldn't do. Allisee still wasn't sure if the woman had outgrown her teenage years. The elf couldn't relate to the fast growth of humans. The archer lifted her necklace pouch to her lips and kissed it. "People call some places 'Hell.' Even this place can be one. I saw Hell. This isn't it. Nay fear here." She tapped her heart as she finished.

Allisee nodded and smiled at each of her partners. "If you know me for long, you'll find I prefer to talk my way through struggles." She tried to decide how best to phrase her next words without giving away too much. "As you've already seen, when I'm pushed, I release the storm I hold inside."

Vallese met Cruso's glance but said nothing. She didn't trust magic, and they witnessed how the elf had unleashed and shredded her victims. The archer wondered how much Allisee 'held inside.'

Urgosk and Sir Cruso led the way, side-by-side, down the hall. They could hear sounds of fighting, though the tunnel echoes made it difficult to get a sense of direction. Nevertheless, Urgosk believed he knew the way they needed to go.

The tunnels became more complex, more open, more criss-crossed by several byways, bridges and stairs. They knew they were moving within the heart of the orc stronghold, so they moved carefully. Orc voices came from everywhere. The companions stuck to shadows when possible. At one point, a large contingent of orc warriors charged across a wooden span passing over their heads. Luckily, the enemies seemed so intent on their course that none looked down.

Passing another side-tunnel, Sir Cruso put up a hand to stop the rest. "Look there," he whispered urgently.

"Humans," Mornik agreed.

A figure, struck dead, lay in the passage. Though stained, the human bore a cloak of light blue and had dropped a shield bearing a red, two-headed griffin. Beyond him, though partly obstructed, they could see an ongoing fight between orcs and similarly dressed humans.

Sir Cruso began to step that direction. Urgosk held him back. "We want the noble." The half-orc insisted as the knight stared daggers down at him. "Kashmer may be here, but the noble'll be dead before they reach 'im."

The human gave a wistful look back down the hall before nodding and agreeing with Urgosk. "You are right. It's just not in my nature to skirt around a fight."

The half-orc led them into another junction. "Think he's around…"

A roar interrupted him. A pair of orc warriors attacked Vallese, and she was already reacting to the attack. Her staff swung, knocking twice in rapid succession as she diverted their weapons. Focused on the quick kill, they continued pressing her. She couldn't accomplish more than hold her defense, until the head of Heel ascended between the legs of one of the orcs. The orc stood tall for a moment before shortening right down to the floor. Vallese battered the remaining orc's maul, nearly pinning it to the wall. An iron dagger, Cruso's specialty weapon against fey creatures, spun over the woman and sank into the warrior's shoulder. The stunned orc let go of its weapon with one hand, leaving it vulnerable. Vallese spun and jabbed, knocking teeth out.

The archer reached out and plucked Cruso's weapon. Thinking better of it, she paused to stick the orc once more in the chest. There was no time to savor the opponent falling down.

"They found us! Forward!" The knight yelled.

Vallese couldn't hand back the dagger; Cruso already fought a new enemy blocking their path. She quickly wiped it on an orc tapestry featuring rather mortifying artwork. It depicted an orc chieftain overseeing his tribe feasting on headless corpses. Vallese looked away and stuck the dagger in her belt.

The knight had a difficult time with this newest opponent. Against most orcs, Cruso had the advantage in reach. This orc used the benefit of the wider tunnel to wield a spear, stabbing relentlessly. Cruso kept his shield tucked close. Between his shifting shield and his armor, the orc didn't have many openings. When the knight feigned an overreaching strike, the orc lunged at the torso. It was a move Cruso had been trained to perform. The spear scratched along the knight's breastplate at too shallow an angle to penetrate. Meanwhile, Cruso shifted the shield, grabbing the haft with his left hand still tucked into the shield strap. Momentarily trapped, the orc couldn't back away fast enough as the steel sword jabbed true.

Both combatants dropped the spear as Cruso pressed the attack. The bastard sword skewered the orc a second time, leaving him curled on the floor. Cruso and Urgosk forced their way into the wider tunnel. The half-orc picked up the spear, hurling it at another orc entering their view. He missed, but the lone orc opponent back up anyway. The disciplined knight, moving through measured stances effortlessly, pressed him hard on one side. The raging berserker approached the other side, Urgosk's eyes looking wild and spit flying from his mouth in a roar. A rush of pain hit the orc. Within moments, the orc lay staring at the ceiling, hardly registering the parting sting from a thin, elf blade.

The five companions rushed into the upper level of a large chamber. They found themselves upon a wide ledge, looking down into a bloody skirmish on the level below. Ranks of armored orcs pressed against the red griffin shields of human armsmen. The armsmen did not display Kashmer's standard, leaving the companions puzzled. The humans, sorely outnumbered but supported by wizards and priests, tried desperately to hold back the tide of axes and serrated cleavers.

Urgosk's eyes turned to the others. They could see the mad rage burning in those yellow-and-red orbs. "Across the way!"

His target: a wide ledge on the other end of a small leap. A simple bridge had once connected these two nearby prominences. The tattered remains of ropes and boards marked its recent demise. They would have to jump a gap spanning over the heads of the orc hordes. From their perspective, but not so apparent to the humans below, a well-dressed and decorated orc observed the fight and shouted orders from the opposite ledge.

The half-orc didn't even wait for the others before flying over the gap as the lone orc captain drew a toothed sword and raised his shield in defense. Sir Cruso charged and jumped for the far end. One boot slipped on the edge as he landed, momentum carrying him to safety. Taking quick stock of Urgosk's fight, the knight worried more for the safety of his other companions. After all, Urgosk could handle himself well. Cruso threw down his sword and shield and put his attention on the others.

Allisee hit the ledge stomach-first. Her sword skittered forward as her hands clutched for a hold. Fine elf legs kicked just over the heads of orc pikes. She winced as she felt a weapon slam against one calf. The protective shield enacted by her wand earlier remained in place, preventing the loss of her limb. Cruso grabbed hold and nearly ripped her arm from its socket as he pulled. The knight's strength yanked her out of trouble. She landed with a roll on the ledge.

Urgosk brought all the power of his swing at the enemy shield. The orc captain angled his shield to partially deflect the blow, leaving Urgosk dangerously extended. He impulsively twisted away just enough that the enemy sword scratched only a shallow reply in his side.

Allisee screamed at the orc captain as she closed. He turned to deal with this new threat, only to witness her whirl out of striking distance. The diversion gave Urgosk the time he needed to recover.

Mornik looked across the impossible distance the elf had narrowly cleared. He knew he couldn't make the jump.

Vallese stepped to the edge. One of her hands tucked into a pocket and spoke a few hushed words. Her dark brown eyes sought him as she extended a hand. "I can help."

Mornik belted Heel and strapped his shield over his back. He could see Cruso awaiting the attempt, hands outstretched. Beyond him, Allisee and Urgosk continued trying to maneuver and flank their skilled opponent.

The dwarf cursed, "Goblin breath!"

He charged toward the edge, fully confident that he was about to land in the throng of orcs below. He reached Vallese and joined hands. She bounced a step with him. As he kicked his legs, she pulled on his arm. Whatever magic the woman possessed, she had more strength than her human frame displayed.

Despite Vallese's aid, he still fell short.

Cruso's arms shot out, catching Mornik as he hit the ledge similar to Allisee's attempt. The shorter, armored legs proved less vulnerable to the pikes below. He kicked furiously as he tried to climb. Cruso went red in the face from the effort of trying to haul the dwarf onto the ledge.

Vallese backed a few feet from the edge. She slipped a hand into her pocket, touching the familiar tuft of hair. *Grace of the panther.* Despite Cruso and Mornik struggling at the other edge, Vallese ran and jumped.

The orc captain had a hard time keeping his opponents from threatening him from opposite sides. He backed into a corner, keeping both his attackers where he could see them. Urgosk carried most of the attack. He roared in full berserker rage as his axe swung deadly arcs. Allisee feared to venture too close. She lacked the swordsmanship of their opponent. The enemy managed to sidestep or deflect everything the half-orc offered.

Urgosk's rage worked against him. In one swift motion, the orc captain locked their weapons together and shoulder-slammed Urgosk to the ground. He left his back open to Allisee. Knowing she had to intervene, she lunged at the captain's back. The elf realized the ruse a moment later as her sword found only air. The orc, spinning to the side, ignored the downed berserker and attacked Allisee.

His sword tip jabbed between her breasts.

The field provided by her magic wand denied the captain from skewering her. It still allowed the force of the blow to knock the sorceress flat. Allisee had a feeling the magic field was gone unless she could use the wand again, but the teeth of the orc's sword hacked down. She barely got her blade in-line to deflect it. He used his favorable leverage to angle her sword away.

His boot stomped on her right arm. Allisee felt an explosion of pain from her elbow. It blocked out the nerves in her hand, and she saw her sword fall out of her grip. He raised his sword for another blow.

She pointed a finger from her free hand. Straining to gather the energy for a spell, she uttered, "Lillon!"

An electric bolt fired into him. Exhausted, the magic stunned Allisee for about as long as it took for the orc to shake it off.

Urgosk charged in, axe swinging. The captain recovered his wits just in time. Still standing on the elf's arm, he ducked the charge. Urgosk rolled off to the side, cursing loudly. The orc blade raised to finish Allisee. She lacked the strength for anymore tricks.

The serrated sword swiped down. A staff intercepted it as a dark form jumped over the elf. Vallese slammed into his cheek with the tail end of her weapon. The leather-skinned orc shrugged off the blow and still managed to swipe his shield across. The edge of it caught Vallese in the head, scratching a cut across her brow.

As the captain maneuvered, Allisee rolled aside. She managed to snag her hilt with her offhand, holding it awkwardly. Her useless right arm tucked against her belly.

Vallese's staff darted in twice, deflected once by the sword and again by the shield. The captain stepped back as Urgosk launched into him again. This time, the raging half-orc tempered his attack. Urgosk's axe tore a long hole in the shield.

Allisee approached from a third side. The elf knew she couldn't contribute much. She'd never really carried the sword in her left hand, and she knew the captain outmatched her hand-to-hand skills.

As the orc captain confidently faced the three opponents, he taunted Urgosk in the orc tongue, but a steel bastard sword ended it prematurely, sweeping the orc's head over the ledge and into the swarm on the lower level. Sir Cruso stepped over the fallen opponent. Mornik followed, slamming Heel into the headless corpse.

Allisee cocked an eyebrow Mornik's way, "You thought he might get up again?"

The dwarf cradled her sore arm and offered her a healing potion. "Nay, but it's hard to break a habit."

Although the elf and dwarf shared a moment of levity, Urgosk took matters a step farther. The half-orc, grunting in rage, picked up the body and cast it into the throng of angry orcs beneath the ledge. He shouted something in the orc tongue. A few thrown spears forced the half-orc to back away from the edge. Eyes wild, he grabbed a large rock and threw it at the enemy.

"Calm! It done!" Vallese yelled at Urgosk.

The half-orc didn't seem to hear. His breath remained hurried, tusks bared to bite, eyes roaming for a target. Sir Cruso stepped into his view. The knight's words got full attention.

"It isn't over, and they can follow us! You said we are almost there…lead on!"

Urgosk roared as he faced the exit. He raised his axe and proclaimed, "First Hand!"

Cruso turned and spotted Vallese's confused expression. He whispered, "His rage is all that keeps him upright."

Vallese could see that he spoke the truth. As she had witnessed earlier, weariness stole at all their movements. Urgosk darted away, the rest moving quickly to follow. The half-orc trailed blood as he sprinted. Sir Cruso hadn't even bothered to wipe his sword, which also left a trail. Vallese tried wiping her eyes clear of her newest wound. Allisee kept the sword in her offhand as she sprinted. As usual, her clothes were still drenched red from her enemies. Mornik jaunted after them, repeating 'breathe' as if it was Nandorrin's holy mantra.

A couple of turns brought them to a lengthy staircase that circled up to a higher room. A second set of a few steps descended into a room below the first. They could hear fighting echoing from somewhere distant. The source seemed to originate from the upper exit.

They had the briefest glimpse of figures in the upper room. Two orcs wore dress and ornamentation that spoke volumes about their rank; clearly beyond ordinary warriors. A third figure held their gaze, for the brief time he could be seen. The companions saw only the human's fine attire, despite bearing rips and stains. He had to be their goal. The attention of all three mostly focused a different direction.

All five companions stopped briefly, glancing into the scene but seeing only the orc general speaking to someone they couldn't view. However, one of the commanding orcs did turn and notice the companions, pausing long enough to bark a command. Several warriors charged out from the upper chamber, joining ranks of guards already blocking the rising stairs.

Urgosk's rage overruled proper judgment. The berserker threw himself at the guards lined across the bottom of the stairs. The orcs were only holding a line, but Urgosk's advance forced them to fight.

Vallese cursed as Urgosk charged impossible odds. The group knew he was leading them toward their doom.

Cruso paced alongside the crazy half-orc. "We can't get up this way!"

The knight's shield rose in defense. Counterblows directed at the half-orc sparked across the yellow/green heraldry. On the opposite side, a red/gold shield bearing Nandorrin's flames deflected more hits. Clashing metal and war cries reverberated off the cavern walls. Urgosk roared and continuously hacked overhead at the enemy. To either side, his human and dwarf companions focused more on defensive measures to keep them alive.

Allisee and Vallese tucked closely behind the others. Both women could see a larger problem forming.

The archer called out, "More behind," as a few orcs came from the same passage they just vacated.

"Bows above," the elf declared as she tried to draw her wand with her injured arm.

The sorceress silently pleaded for the wand to have charges left as she pointed it into her skin and spoke the command. Mornik's recent healing potion barely touched her newest injuries. Above, several orcs on the stairway had a clear view of her. As the magic took hold, Allisee stepped protectively in front of Vallese and stretched her arms wide. She picked out a word she believed Urgosk and other orcs had been using as a curse during their fighting, shouting it at the bowmen.

A rain of arrows pelted her. The wave seemed to bounce away, but it still took Allisee a precious moment to realize she still lived. At her side, the males shifted.

Cruso shouted, "Right! To the door! Move!"

The knight continued to shout and push, redirecting the group to the lower room exit. Mornik turned his efforts, passing the elf as he used Heel to create an opening.

The half-orc roared, "He's up there!"

"Find another way!" Cruso shoved the berserker.

Despite the room filling with orcs, only two guards blocked the open door to the lower chamber. The group's desperation-fueled attacks slammed both orcs aside. Allisee funneled a feeble jolt into one. The effort made her swoon, and she sprawled across the room's entry.

Vallese reached down, pulling the limp sorceress despite an arrow lodging in her thigh. Mornik overran the other orc, noting the open doors of this chamber and an internal locking bar.

"We can bar this door!"

Cruso had his back to the new room, slowly retreating to it as his armored body defended against the pursuing orcs. Urgosk stood his ground next to the man, axe blade chopping in wide sweeps.

The knight clung to his code of honor. To Mornik he said, "I will give you space. Bar it and find safety."

"There will be no sacrifices here!" The dwarf shouted. "I'll clear them, you two be ready to slam the doors!"

Cruso and Urgosk found it difficult to hold back the press of bodies as Mornik moved between them. Mornik threw his shield and weapon behind him.

"Feel Nandorrin's fury!" He roared.

He began a prayer while thrusting both arms forward. Vallese, crouched over the fallen sorceress, remembered the miracle and the furnace warmth it generated earlier. The air before him distorted as his blast hit the line of orcs. Even Cruso and Urgosk flinched from the heat. The front three orcs darkened as their exposed possessions caught fire. Their hair ignited in flames, skin cracked and darkened. Arrow fletchings sticking out of quivers burst aflame. Unlit wall sconces suddenly lit. A fan of flames rose with the heat up the stairwell winding above. The crowd of attackers reeled from the fire, throwing hands up and seeking cover.

As the miracle expired, Mornik stumbled backward. His eyes rolled back, followed by the rest of his body as he passed out on his back.

Cruso and Urgosk were already throwing the doors closed. The knight noticed the orc-blood's hands trembling. His rage had played out. Vallese limped over to help. She lent a hand despite her own limbs shaking. Together, they managed to slam the bar into place.

*

Both Allisee and Mornik lie sprawled on the floor, lost in their dreams. The remaining three had a chance to further examine this new room, which they'd only glimpsed during combat. Large and dark, rows of support beams held up a cracked ceiling. Horizontal boards stretched between support pillars, shoring up the weakened chamber. Straw and grass matted the floor. From the smell and noises ahead, they realized this room corralled animals. Sconces, whether arcane or divine, lit the room at intervals. This ensured a live flame couldn't get knocked over and set any fires amongst the straw. The far end of the room housed cages containing a few large wolves similar to the ones who pulled the war chariot. Closer to the entry, stood several grazing animals that neither Cruso nor Vallese recognized.

"What are those?" The knight asked.

Urgosk stumbled closer to the animal pens. "Umdroos. Never seen 'em?" At the shake of their heads, he continued. "Pack beasts from the Deeprealm. Similar to a cow, not quite as tasty. Milk, cheese, steaks. Also used as draft animals."

Umdroos looked nothing like a cow, other than being bulky, hairy, and smelly. These creatures stretched longer than a cow, but moved more closely to the ground on thick legs.

Cruso hardly looked over the beasts because the few large wolves at the opposite end of the room worried him. Those pens included vertical posts reinforcing them. His main concern, however, remained his companions. Mornik snored as if sleeping on a luxury bed. Graceful Allisee lie crumpled in a heap. Vallese sat near both, her leg outstretched and staring at the arrow lodged in it.

The knight waved to get her attention. "Search them. They may yet bear a healing draught."

"The dwarf," she spoke as she swiveled her leg to move. "Once awake, he heal?"

Cruso shook his head. His sweat-drenched hair clung to his face. "They will find nay benefit from such a miracle. Nor would he be capable of another miracle in his state. They are drained of spirit. Rest is what they require. I hope you can find a potion in one of their bags to heal your leg. The orcs will soon…"

Before he could finish, a loud bang shook the entry door. "They found a ram!" He glanced at the cracked ceiling. "Either they will break the door or bring the roof down on us. I see nay exit!"

From inside the pens, Urgosk called out. "Droppin' the roof sounds like a plan!"

"What are you doing?"

"Umdroos' bones are packed with meat, an' they gots wolves to drive 'em."

Another impact shook the door.

A surprised exclamation erupted from Vallese. "I found one!"

Cruso quick-stepped to the woman's side. He grabbed firmly onto the arrow, staring into her dark eyes. She nodded. The knight pulled the shaft. Her scream diminished under another boom rocking the door. The noise encouraged her to action. She drank the last draught dry, revitalizing her as it healed her wounds from the inside.

Their half-orc companion ran from pen to pen, carrying harnesses. "Git Sparks and Torch to this side! An' help me!"

Vallese's brow crinkled in confusion, "Sparks? Torch?"

Cruso answered, "He's given us nicknames. You're Sticks."

"Sticks!?"

Another ramming strike cracked one of the door boards. Urgosk yelled, "Hurry!"

The knight hoisted the dwarf over his shoulders, grimacing under the underestimated weight. He staggered a weaving line to the back. Vallese wrapped her arms under Allisee's shoulders, dragging the elf and her blood-stained garb through straw and worse. Both indisposed companions were propped against the back wall, near the wolves.

The knight huffed after setting Mornik down. "Won't the wolves be a risk?"

Urgosk voice sounded weary, "Nay. They'll chase the 'droos."

Cruso began to note Urgosk's handiwork. "You're crazy."

"Been a crazy week!"

The knight pointed at the ceiling, "But bringing the roof…"

"There's another floor up there, and the noble is above us! Just makin' a new tunnel."

Barely a minute later, the locking bar shattered under a ramming blow. Sundered shards fell inward. Orcs roared in victory as they rushed the entry. Pike blades led the way, hoisted by arms splashed with war paint. Serrated swords and large, curved axes waved behind the front chargers. In the dim light, the variously colored orc eyes stood out. Some berserkers led, frothing until they spilled drool as they ran. Their chieftain had been killed and hostage lost, but they still had a chance to spill Kashmer blood. Anger mixed with the taste of vengeance.

On the other side of a line of freed umdroos, Urgosk and Sir Cruso raised whips. The beasts already had reason to sense fear. Vallese had teased and proffered some bits of their hair to the wolf cages in the rear. The wolves didn't require much prompting to hunger for fresh umdroo meat. Vallese began withdrawing the pins securing the cages. The wolves clawed and gnashed at the bars. Both men began cracking the whips over the heads of the hearty draft creatures. They shouted at the charging orcs.

"First Hand!"

"Dalios count you!"

The stampede began in earnest. Umdroos charged for the only exit to the room, heedless of the orcs. One umdroo, then another, felt resistance on their harnesses. Urgosk had connected them to stretch between the animals and snag on the numerous support poles holding up the cracked ceiling.

Vallese rattled the pins. The bottom tips barely kept the excited wolves in check, but sent a clear signal to the umdroos. The beasts drew on their strength and instincts.

The charging orcs slowed as they began to understand what lay ahead.

The first beam snapped. A second one slipped from its base. The umdroos barely hesitated as their collective bulk swept through beam after beam. Chunks of rock began falling around the missing supports. The umdroos' panic worsened as the cage pins finally slipped free. Vallese fell back behind the swinging doors as the large wolves barreled ahead. They howled in fury, charging amidst falling rocks and dust. The umdroos desperately pushed to the exit. Rows of thick beams snapped and toppled.

The three Kashmer-sent adventurers sought safety even as the entire continent felt like it rained around them. Vallese swung into a cage once the wolves evacuated it. She hoped that its framework would hold. *I'm an animal among people, anyway.*

Sir Cruso staggered through bouncing stones, his raised shield deflecting several. Upon seeing the danger falling around the unconscious elf, he discarded the whip. The back wall fared well so far, and the rain of debris lessened there. The knight threw himself and his shield protectively over her body. His free arm hugged her close. Cruso thought he could still detect a hint of her perfume despite the unpleasant smells acquired through the day. He looked into Allisee's peaceful expression as she slept. It was a breathtaking contrast to the weight of the world attempting to crush his shield onto both of them.

Urgosk practically flew through a veil of rocks on his own route to the back. The downfall eased slightly near Mornik's spot by the wall. The half-orc reached down and grabbed the flame-decorated shield. Instead of properly covering the dwarf, Urgosk turned and sat down on him. He propped the shield over his head. As long as the world was ready to drop on him, the half-orc enjoyed his upright seat as he watched the ending. He lost sight of their hosts. Orcs and animals alike faded behind a storm of falling stone.

*

Despite a fog of dust, new light streamed into the animal room from the altar room above. Once the rocks settled, the stampede of animals could still be heard running in the distance, and no orc war cries filled the air.

Urgosk looked to his right. Vallese shakily got to her feet. The metal cage protected her, but the half-orc realized it had warped. The woman began wrenching at the stuck door. He moved to assist, tilting the dwarf's shield so that a clatter of stones fell to the side. Glancing left, he saw Sir Cruso picking himself up from Allisee. The sorceress' breathing could be heard, despite the snoring coming from their healer.

"What devilry was this?" Called a voice from overhead.

The companions looked up to notice an armored man peering down from the ruined floor above. His vestments and decorative armor advertised wealth, and he stood with regal bearing. Soldiers accompanied him along the rim, their blue-and-red heraldry matched those of the private armsmen they witnessed earlier.

It occurred to Cruso who these people must be. "The Regindal family," he whispered in awe.

The man's attention focused on the nearby rocks. "Lord Felnick! How does he fare?"

Knight and half-orc noticed a dust-covered figure lying amidst the rubble. Both climbed over the rocks to reach him, while Vallese stubbornly tried forcing the cage door.

"Orc!" A soldier in the upper room cried, leveling a crossbow.

117

Cruso threw his hands wide. "He's a Kashmer privateer! We arrived with the navy!"

The lead figure motioned his armsman to lower the crossbow, "The navy has barely left the shoreline!"

Urgosk showed his unarmed hands. "They couldn't keep up, so we left 'em."

The men on the upper level tried to figure a safe way down. Cruso went to the fallen man and exhaled relief to discover he still breathed. "He lives. Tell me, is this indeed Lord Felnick Pentle?"

"*Privateer*," The noble leading the armsmen sneered, "You are addressing *Lord* Archem Regindal. Aye, that nobleman is our quest."

Urgosk cracked a smile as he stood and addressed those above. "Ah, yer just in time!"

"In time?"

The half-orc smiled. "In time to witness us rescue Lord Fentle!"

Cruso hissed, "Lord *Felnick Pentle*!"

Urgosk shrugged at the knight, "Well, they know who he is." He turned his smiling tusks on the nobleman above him. "Who do we return him to fer our land claim?"

Lord Archem of the Regindals glowered at the half-orc.

Volume 1, Chapter 9   **1 pitcher, 2 mugs and 2 glasses**

"Why 'Sticks'?" Vallese asked, glaring over the rim of a dented drinking mug.

"Ya use sticks!" Urgosk's drink-augmented bellow easily carried to the next table of the tavern. "A blunt one, bent one, lots of little pointed ones. Sticks you are!"

Vallese, fuming, looked over at her other table companion. Sir Cruso shrugged, "He stuck me with the nickname 'Paladin,' which I shall point out is erroneous as well."

Her eyebrows raised. "But, you are holy warrior, are you not?"

"Nay. I may appear very pious, but I don't channel divine miracles as paladins do. My training is purely martial..." Sir Cruso continued talking, trying to speak over the background noise.

The dark-skinned women leaned in close to hear him over the tavern noises. Yetrayal's Hold was one of the noisiest establishments of libations in Kashmer. The curses of sailors droned endlessly, interrupted by exclamations from the gambling tables. Music from low-wage musicians occasionally made it past the screen of vulgarities. The interrupted notes that reached their ears gave the impression of good tunes. Occasional laughter flowed from those enjoying the 'companionship' offered by the establishment as a side-revenue.

Despite the background noise, Cruso finished his lengthy explanation. "…since the Covenant bars the gods from taking any direct hand in our world, only those priests and paladins willing to train and channel that energy can act as their representatives. However, while I respect a number of teachings, my devotion doesn't extend that far. In Diara, I was trained to rise to my father's position. Usually the third son or second daughter would be sent to the church. I may have faith, but it's not part of my weaponry."

"Which son?" Vallese asked. At Cruso's confused look, she added. "You first? Second?"

Cruso's eyes saddened, lowering until they found his mug. He took a drink before answering. "Second. The second son trains in martial weapons and horsemanship, but generally with less responsibilities than the oldest. Until two years ago, when my brother succumbed to a strange illness. After that, I was raised to be the heir."

"Yer a long way from yer daddy's lands." Urgosk spoke with one raised eyebrow.

Cruso grimly responded, "Not everything goes as planned."

He spoke despite the distraction across the table. Although Vallese had stuffed herself into a corner, a leering sailor managed to 'stumble' and get a hand on her. She shoved the man back into the crowd with much more force than he likely expected.

The woman scowled at the half-orc. "You do not pick next inn, if there is next inn."

Cruso agreed with Vallese, though he realized the woman also didn't understand how provocative her attire remained. The knight, freed from the threat of battle, wore fine clothes but no armor as he drank. Vallese, however, continued to wear her leather corset. The woman didn't understand how its design brought attention to her best attributes rather than offer much protection. She needed an education in true armor, as well as fashion modesty.

Their conversation further stalled when they heard a loud yelp across the bar. High-pitched, it carried the length of the tavern. It was quickly followed by raucous laughter and drowned in music.

Cruso took another sip from his mug. "Milady, I believe if you have the coin, I should help you find a proper armory."

Two new arrivals drifted to the empty seats at the table even as Cruso finished speaking. Both Allisee and Mornik frowned as they sat. The elf took the same tactic as Vallese, tucking herself beside the wall.

The half-orc pounded the table. "Ah! Our slick-tongues return, hopefully with shiny medals and the proper land title!"

The dwarf spoke, though his words were aimed at Allisee. "What happened a moment ago?"

"He touched me in an unsuitable way," her cerulean eyes glanced back into the crowd, where the earlier ruckus had been heard. She held up two fingers and a spark jumped between them. "So I touched *him* in an unsuitable way."

Chuckling, the Nandorrin priest pointed at the table pitcher before indicating his own fragile glass. "If I'd known there was a pitcher handy, I might have held out for that."

Sir Cruso grinned. "Urgosk claims the entire pitcher for himself."

Vallese interpreted the countenance both new arrivals wore when they approached. Mornik and Allisee had been gone for hours. "Bad news," she declared.

The elf nodded. She took a sip from her wine glass before continuing. "I tried. Lord Felnick doesn't even remember us. He clearly remembers the Regindals freeing him before the collapse. Kashmer's Army officers witnessed the Regindals spearheading the attack, even bringing some giant conjuration that opened a hole into the tunnels."

"Did the navy have a say in anything?" The knight inquired.

Mornik set his glass down and spat his words, "Said they thought we were dead or deserters. They hadn't seen us."

The other three rose in their chairs but the elf extended a restraining hand. "We were hailed for our efforts in the end. One of the Regindals, a priest of Dawn, spoke highly of us. I think it upset his family, but he honored us for our bravery and skill. Some attendees were impressed by our effort."

Urgosk threw his hands wide, "But nay reward! Nay gate-front quench house?"

Allisee shook her head. "The Regindals are of noble blood, and highly regarded in Kashmer. We are...mostly non-human privateer peons."

Over Allisee's words, the others barely heard Vallese ask, "Quench-house?" Followed by Cruso pointing at his mug.

The table dropped silent as a buxom serving girl approached Urgosk, a fresh pitcher in hand. "Urgosk, are you sharing any with your friends?"

The half-orc wrapped a hand around her waist. Although the companions lost sight of it, she gave a squeal and a slight jump. "I handle a pitcher or two jus' fine. I might even hunger fer something more when the candles git low."

The girl tittered and ran a finger suggestively over his thick arm muscles before departing with his empty pitcher. Aware of the table's eyes on him, Urgosk returned to the topic at the table, "We git anything extra? We put in a lot o' risk fer the city."

"Standard muster wages," Allisee responded. "We got paid for serving our time, that's all. That doesn't even cover recharging my wand."

"Or used potions," Mornik lamented.

"A shame that our actions and risks went unrewarded." Sir Cruso shook his head. "You tried your best. Nobility rules as it pleases."

Allisee sensed a deeper meaning behind those words, since Sir Cruso descended from nobility. Or did he? The sorceress silently admitted that there was little she knew of her companions except their dependability. *And their ability to survive crazy plans*, she amended silently.

"As I said, we impressed folks, including nobility in attendance." She spoke, "Such prestige has the side-effect of generating new offers. They know where to contact me, and how to message those of you who actually are privateers."

They began to notice Urgosk rummaging through something under the table. The half-orc passed a sack to Vallese, keeping it below the tabletop and out of sight. "Those 'papers' I acquired should salvage something for our efforts."

He looked at Allisee as he spoke, so Vallese continued to pass the sack under the table. The archer couldn't resist peeking down, and gasped as she did. The sack went to Allisee, and she held it between Mornik and herself as she stole a glance. It felt too heavy to contain 'papers'.

The elf and dwarf put forth legendary effort in not giving away their awe of what lay inside. The bawdry tavern had no shortage of eyes and ears that could pick out wealth. Urgosk's bag brimmed with sparkly objects. Gold and silver, rings and jewelry. Not everything looked expensive, but altogether it would replace their investments. Mornik finished passing the bag around the table. The knight's eyes went wide, darted inquisitively at his companions, then once again feasted on the glint of coins.

The elf sipped her glass. Judging by her bouncing feet and tapping fingers, the drink was the only thing pausing a cascade of questions. She couldn't resist holding back for long. "Ok, how?"

Urgosk glanced around at all the possible eavesdroppers in the room. "Let's grab a room."

Mornik huffed, "Do we have to put in more cash for a room I won't sleep in?"

The half-orc winked, "You can rent rooms by the hour here."

Allisee glanced over Yetrayal's Hold's clientele, "I find myself unsurprised."

*

"It's a reflexive response whenever an enemy hits the ground," Urgosk explained in privacy.

The cramped quarters held only a cot, coat hooks, and a shoddy chair. Despite this, the companions managed to squeeze in without anyone sitting in the middle of the stained and smelly mattress. No one sat in the chair either, but Cruso used it as a footrest as he leaned his back to the bolted door.

The half-orc continued, "He falls, my hand snaps out, grabs the coin-bag, plops it in a sack. Move on ta the next enemy. The rest of ya weren't fallin' quickly enough on purses at the end of those scraps, so I took it upon meself."

"Orcs carried all this?" The incredulous elf sorted through the jewelry in Urgosk's sack.

"Nay, I also libery-ated…libbyate…"

"Liberated?" Asked Cruso.

"Pfft, aye. When I went sneakin' 'round, found lots of goodies tucked in places. Couldn't leave 'em there."

Vallese huffed, "We waited, scared, every time you scouted. You looted?"

The half-orc only grinned as he threw up his hands. "Where would we be now without it? Nay reward. Nay special thanks fer our work."

"We?" Sir Cruso nodded towards the bag, "So you will share?"

"I'm loyal to mah tribe. We got through, we all gets paid!"

The knight gave the half-orc a strong pat on the back. "Thank you, for looking out for us."

Vallese piped in from her squatting position in the corner. "Thanks for us surviving crazy plans." She seemed sincere.

"Speaking of which," Allisee closed the bag and handed it back to Urgosk. "What was everyone's plans before Kashmer conscripted us?"

Sir Cruso folded his arms over his chest. "Making a living in exile, or at least attempting to do so. My biggest talents are fighting skills." He paused for a breath and a sigh. "I looked to the arena, but it just seems too…barbaric. My noble blood in Diara counts for little in Kashmer's Protectorate. I have some skills in smithing so that I might maintain my armor and weaponry, but I don't favor becoming a smith's apprentice if I can avoid it. My life's training would feel wasted."

Sir Cruso turned to face Mornik. "Do I still owe someone a life-debt?"

The dwarf waved away the suggestion. "You kept me from dropping into the orcs when I jumped the gap in the tunnel. You also kept me alive after I passed out. We're 'even stones'."

Noticing the knight's puzzled look, Mornik held his hands out, palms up. He mimicked the motion of a merchant's scale balancing both sides, "Even stones. Nay debt."

Cruso nodded and continued speaking to the group. "The privateers were painted in a rather romantic notion to my ears. I signed up hoping to find good company. The recent involuntary muster of swords by Kashmer has left a bad taste to it, but I still hope to find good people and serve the privateers from a bit more distance."

His brown eyes looked wistfully at the elf as he finished. Maybe he predicted her motives for asking.

Legs tucked up against her in a corner, Vallese spoke in her strange accent. "I seek home. Out there, don't know where. Any step takes me closer or farther. I search." She idly toyed with the spirit pouch hanging from her neck.

When nothing more came forth, Urgosk looked to Cruso and pointed at him. "Yer takin' the whole exile sentence too seriously."

"What do you know of it? And who says I was 'sentenced'?"

"I'm in exile too!" Urgosk proclaimed as a proud boast. "My skills are sim'lar ta yers. Life is good, and a good life is the trophy I'm chasin'. You might try strongarm work like me. I can get ya into a local tap. You bust up rowdies and get plenty ta drink."

Straightening his worn vest, Sir Cruso replied, "I believe our tastes for fun differ."

"Yer loss," the half-orc shrugged. "Music and drinks host me ev'ry night. I dance to the rowdiest salt songs those deckhands bring to town. Those boats heading to sea leave a lot of lonely women at the docks…"

The knight ventured, "And what of the First Hand? You left them behind?"

Urgosk's playful atmosphere dropped, uncovering a sneer. "None alive were left behind."

"Please," Allisee interrupted. "I just seek a simple answer to a question." The elf had been holding her hands outward, waving them palms down to calm down the group. She turned to Mornik, laying one hand on his shoulder and facing him with curious eyes. "What of you, Priest Heavyboot?"

Mornik stroked his beard before answering, "I seek something. I'm barred from saying what. I have little to go on except research and exploration. With each new bit of knowledge, my feet will find their proper path."

"My words would mirror yours," the sorceress admitted. "Have you found a direction?"

Like Allisee and Cruso, Mornik also cleaned up well since their adventure, especially since he accompanied Allisee in the attempt to impress Kashmer's nobility. Unlike Cruso, he wore his armor and Nandorrin-symbol tabard.

Mornik stroked his beard as he answered. "I've found some journals that may help, but I'm still studying them. Not sure where they will lead yet. And you?"

Allisee's brow wrinkled, "Truthfully, I need help with my next step, which is why I inquired of your plans."

As Allisee paused, she could tell she had their attention. They looked or leaned closer to her. "Sir Cruso asked why I was wounded and recovering at Monastery of The Codex. I wasn't willing to share that tale earlier. Perhaps now is the time."

She glanced at each of them in turn. All of them patiently awaited her tale. "I also seek old journals that may give me answers to my questions. The answers lie in a ruined castle; a rather short expedition just up the coast."

"How old are the ruins?" Sir Cruso asked.

"It was attacked 350 years ago. Though it was looted, the attackers failed to take everything."

Urgosk picked at his tusks, "Must 'ave been looted more times afterward."

She nodded, "But the adventurers who've gone there have had their share of troubles as well. I've seen written accounts. Danger still clings to the area. It hasn't given up all its secrets."

Mornik wore a suspicious frown, barely visible over the beard. "How do you *know* treasures remain? Why wasn't it all looted centuries ago?"

"A survivor still lives. An old elf, living in Thellistae." The others revealed surprise, perhaps forgetting about the longevity of elves. "I trust her tale. There are still rewards worth the trip, and secret ways about the ruins which I have learned. I thought…" Allisee realized she had to pick her words carefully. "…that I had a means to sneak past many of those dangers. I was wrong."

Her eyes beseeched them, "I need help. I need a group that I can trust. My only interest is any writing we find. Scripts, old records, journals. Any valuables you find you can keep and divide amongst yourselves."

Within minutes, Allisee answered their important questions and convinced the rest to join up for another adventure. She didn't have to work hard to sign them up. None of the others seemed to have well-defined plans or any tight schedules. The elf didn't even have to delve into the dangers of the keep, for the others craved proper sleep foremost and preferred to hear more once a good rest cleared their minds.

Not all craved a bed for the same reason. As they left the rented room to leave for their respective rooms in the city, Urgosk lingered. Sir Cruso looked back in time to see the serving wench from downstairs tiptoe down the hall and slip past Urgosk as he held the door.

"I paid for *two* hours," the half-orc winked and closed the door to the rest of them.

The knight suffered the unbidden vision of the serving girl trying to kiss Urgosk's ugly maw. He imagined the displeasure of trying to place lips around such yellow fangs, and shivered.

*

Mornik Heavyboot settled into his room, at a more respectable inn. Despite the late hour, he stoked the fireplace and gathered writing tools. Dipping the quill into the inkpot, he offered a brief prayer to Nandorrin before committing his words to parchment.

Uncle Vermact,

I hope this letter finds the clan well. Their plight is in my prayers every day. Of course, they are at the heart of my pilgrimage.

Doyal has been a month of change. My experience in Kashmer has been mixed blessings and depravations. I became forced to join a crusade on Kashmer's part into the orc-infested hills to the south. Although the time spent may have hindered my search, I don't think anyone there could fault me the opportunity to dent some orc skulls.

The dwarf paused in his writing. He looked about the room for inspiration, until he noticed Heel leaning against his table.

You'll be happy to know that the hammer you blessed, Brozek, smote its share of savages. Sadly, I don't think the orcs will relent those caves easily. We'd need a good century to scrub out their stink.

The best result of this crusade: I seem to have found a capable small-clan. Perhaps not the most trustworthy sort. A pall of mystery hangs over each, yet I am not so different. For obvious reasons, I can't say much about my quest to them. Likewise, they keep closed counsel as well.

A Diaran knight, named Sir Cruso Lanvyrl. I seem most akin with his beliefs and sense of honor. Yet, he may have committed the gravest act in the mindset of both our people and his…he lives in exile. His service has been sundered from whatever lord he once owed fealty. Hopefully I will soon find the truth of why such an honor-bound soldier has forsaken his home.

A human archer, whose skin bears a shade darker than any human I've seen, calling herself Vallese Foxblood. She quests for a lost homeland. Simple enough, except her limited language skills express nay clues as to the long path she's traveled. She possesses strange gifts I've never encountered, augmenting her physical skills to adapt to any situation. Has Vallese ever lived in a large city before Kashmer? She displays social awkwardness. Her eyes and movements seemed more relaxed in the orc hills than in the city. I've seen wicked scars on the inside of her elbow. They stay hidden most of the time. I'm more intrigued by her road than her homeland.

Our best speaker is the elf sorceress, Allisee Lentara. I watched her verbally spar with several human nobles with more grace and aplomb than I possess. Her magical gifts seem wondrous, but I can see sadness within her during unguarded moments. Our next quest is tied to her own search, though where her final goal is directed I have nay clue. She seems capable enough to guide us.

You'll be most surprised to hear of our last companion, a sneaky half-orc named Urgosk.

Mornik had to rest the quill aside for a moment. The proper words to introduce the wild half-orc would not easily form.

He's crazy. Gods have blessed him though, for he's luckier than the average gold miner. His luck paid off for all of us; I'm hoping fate's cards continue to favor him. Like our knight, he also takes pride in a history to which he can't return. Brags about the "First Hand" but has left that group

The dwarf took a few moments perusing the letter. Once done, he stood up and crossed to the fireplace. He tossed the letter into the fire, which utterly consumed it.

Allisee Lentara

Urgosk

Sir Cruso

Vallese Foxblood

Mornik Heavyboot

Appendix A – The Calendar of Dhea Loral

The calendar of Dhea Loral's realm is four hundred days long. That reflects the time it takes for one year to pass for the planet of Epos Goth. The calendar is divided into five seasons, with two months in each season, as follows:

Planting season: Primus, then Florum
Summer season: Jherad, then Doyal
Harvest season: Othgar, then Novak
Waning season: Tiquierum, then Norgrad
Winter season: Vientula, then Icethule

Each month lasts forty days and each week is ten days. The civilized societies of the land do tend to observe two-day weekends; however, much work is still done on these days. The value of a weekend in Dhea Loral is seen more as a time for socializing and public events, but even on these days many merchants are still doing business. There is also a midweek day by which many government offices in the civilized lands take half the day off. The evening on these days feature balls, feasts, religious observations, or other relaxing endeavors. Many people do not observe such luxuries, as the struggle to work and survive has bred a strong work ethic into a number of cultures.

The New Season Day, which commemorates the start of the New Year, is held at the traditional end of winter. Usually it begins to snow in most of the lands by mid to late Norgrad, and by the first of Primus the snow is melting away.

The calendar is measured by an important date in Dhea Loral history. In a time when war swept the lands, several immortals and demigods took sides. Some tried to attain more power, while others defended the realm's inhabitants. Several gods lent their powers to affect the outcome as well. It was a dark time in the world when great civilizations fell and new governments arose. During the waning season of 1 BC, (Before Covenant), the fury of the demigods and the use and destruction of several artifacts led to the destruction of the last great empires. Many races struggled for survival in the winter season that followed. Even those living in the vast cave and underground systems of the world, while not affected by the surface winter, were left weak and foraging for meager provisions. The major powers, those gods who exerted the most influence in the world, stepped in and forced an end to the conflict. On the first of Primus, in the year now called 1 AC, (After Covenant), the gods and demigods signed a pact regarding the involvement of the deities in the future of the world. Although the gods were capable of controlling the world much more directly, restrictions were placed and honored by all. In this way, they voluntarily gave up several privileges, and bound to their oaths. Even the most chaotic of gods can never break the *Covenant*.

This began the modern-day incarnation of the churches and clerics. Clerics became the necessary mortal vessels through which the gods move the races, although the gods retain the necessary powers over nature and magic to make the world run smoothly and stay in balance.

Appendix B – Deities Commonly Worshipped in Dhea Loral

This is not a complete list of all the beings that hold governance over the world of Dhea Loral. It is a glance at some of the major powers that exert their influence over the land, people and natural events. The gods make possible all the little things that keep the world from falling into disharmony. They each have agendas that are carried out by worshippers in the world, for the gods themselves are forbidden to tread the realms as they once did.

Abriana – Goddess of Love and Healing. She is the most loving goddess and a supporter of all that is good and wholesome in the world. She helps instill feelings in mortals of brotherly love, marital commitment, and care of the land. Many of her followers are pacifists and healers. There are others who do take up the call of arms, but only to fight for what they love and protect. Even those that become paladins are restricted from using weapons or incurring fighting on the first day of each month, as these days are sacred to Abriana.

Boyal – God of Justice. It is said when the Goddess of Death collects the souls of agnostics, unbelievers, and those who turned traitor to their god she must bring them before Boyal for sentencing. Once that is done, she is only too happy to carry out the sentence or deliver the wayward soul to its fate. The clerics of this faith often find themselves on city councils, in courtrooms, or even libraries of official records. The concept of law, and how it applies to different people, is carefully studied. Many clerics go on pilgrimages to explore how the cultures of other lands express their laws.

The Codex – Book on the Philosophy of Good. Not a god by itself, it nevertheless has inspired a large following. This way of life is based on a literary work that champions a strong belief in the morals and principles that are known as "good". The original *Codex* was brought into existence with the help of several deities devoted to good causes, and it took a life of its own. People who devote themselves to this following are able to tap into clerical miracles just as if they were praying to a genuine god.

There are many that serve to fulfill the moral requirements set forth in the book.

Daerkfyre – Dwarven god of Strength, Valor and Courage. Worshipped as one of the dwarven "battle gods", this deity favors strong warriors. Daerkfyre is often referred to with the extension "the Valorous". Often worshippers of this god are as strong and stubborn in the mind as they are with their muscles. Physical strength is a domain honored by dwarven miners and certain craftsmen. Warriors often pray to this god before battle. Weapons blessed by his clerics are exceptionally strong and durable.

Dalios – God of War, as well as the humans' God of Strength and Courage. This deity can be wildly unpredictable. At times he sets forth destruction and strife, though sometimes for the benefit of oppressed people. Regardless, this god is a major influence on events that shape the course of the world. His clerics are often eager to go into battle on either side of the lines, and sometimes they do meet across opposite sides of a battlefield. To these clerics, life is met by facing trouble in a straightforward type of manner. The clergy spends their often short lives seeking out glory amidst fighting for a cause. Dalios is believed to look over the world from a huge feasting hall, toasting those who struggle and fight for their beliefs.

Dawn – Goddess of Life and Rebirth. Closely related to Abriana, this goddess shares some of the same ideals. However, this deity views life as chaotic, with a bit of mystery. She creates and shapes new life, from babies to new species. Sometimes the new species can be deadly, but that is only to balance out and strengthen other forms of life. This goddess has a special abhorrence of the undead, and her clerics fight to rid the world of their existence. Due to her zeal for all kinds of life, many of her worshippers include people who feel more at home in nature than in civilized areas built upon stone.

DeLaris – Goddess of Death. Death can never be anything but frightening. She resides in one of the many Lower Worlds, but travels between them often and freely to carry out her tasks. Her most ardent followers in life may pass into the afterworld to become *Karet-Atriul*, otherwise known as Death Angels. These souls become harbingers and servants of her will, assisting the goddess with the many aspects of her position. She ferries the dead across the other worlds and homes of the gods. Those souls who were unfaithful, traitorous to a god, and untrue in their worship may find an eternity of torture or simply a boring, never-ending imprisonment. Some of her most powerful clerics can raise the dead back to life, but only to prove her power over death. Her clerics are not very strong with social ties, for they serve as a constant reminder to others of the dark fates that might befall them in the next world.

Foyul – God of Balance. Foyul works on the principal that too much influence by one side or force tends to imbalance the world. He walks a middle line between anarchy and order, good and evil. His followers come from all walks of life, all serving to sway the balance in their own way when needed. Foyul has few friends among the gods or men, as he tends to fight for all sides in order to not let any one force hold too much sway. His clerics may be evil or good, and may act for any number of good or bad intentions, striving to maintain the balance of the world.

Ganden – God of Honor, Duty, Service. This god has followers in many races. Those that feel fulfilled by a calling of decency to their fellow man and sacrifice for the sake of others fit into his followers. Those who break promises, or serve only themselves, fall out of favor to this deity. Ganden serves the other gods in the same way, carrying out honorable edicts and being of service to those that require aid. Often symbols of this god can be found with militias, honor guards, healers, and others who perform even menial services to others.

Juliustan – God of Storms and Cataclysms. Many races fear the name of this god, without a full understanding of his focus in the worlds. The god has two sides that are apparent to people. On one hand, he strives to balance the natural forces of the world. This can only be done by allowing some of the pressure of the forces of nature to vent their wrath on occasion. He may hold back one storm, while allowing another to rage unchecked. On his other side, he also seeks to ease the suffering of the world's people through such terrible events. This aspect is apparent in his clerics. His followers bring relief to those who have been displaced by storms or cataclysms, and assist in rebuilding. People do not fully understand and tend to fear his name. Many blame him for catastrophes in the first place, and fear that it is somehow anger or wrath. His clerics believe that the world would suffer worse destruction than the Godswars if Juliustan relaxed his control.

Kelor – God of Luck. Although the other gods maintain that followers must have faith, this god prefers blind chance more openly. He champions games of chance, gambling, and random fate. This god tilts the tables in the direction he prefers, so one never knows how chance will turn up. This god rivals Dalios in unexpectedly bringing down great warriors. Many adventurers worship him, or at least pray for his blessing. Clerics of this god often throw themselves at adventure, or raise funds for the church in gambling houses. This god excels in finding small ways to thwart big plans.

Krakus – God of the Sea. The water is home to many creatures, and the oceans and seas have their own unique atmosphere. This god provides a home for some, and can bring down wrath on others with the power of water currents. Sailors pay homage to this god in return for passage over his domain. In time, Krakus can reshape the land with his currents, or smash cities in great waves, (and would do so more often, if not for the interventions of Juliustan). The influence of his domain resulted in several of his churches being built to float out on the water. His clerics have much influence over the element of water and some can walk over its surface.

Laedelious – Elven Goddess of Forests and Wildlands. Commonly referred to as the "Treemother", or "Lady of the Green", this goddess has worked through the elves to further the protection of nature. Due to her guidance, many elves build their cities within the trees and current topography, rather than cut down the woods. Many elves enjoy a certain harmony with the woodland creatures through their history with Laedelious. Though the race of man shapes the land around his needs, elves have learned to shape their civilizations and homes around the needs of nature. Although this goddess has many cleric followers, there are also a number of mystics that work in her name.

Mothrok – Goddess of Earth and Stone. Born of the element of earth, this goddess has a strong connection to earth and stone. She believes in the superiority of everlasting stone, and the plant life that flourishes from the ground. She sees animal life as a type of vermin that infests the planet on which Dhea Loral can be found. Given her perspective, one would think that she would have few followers. In actuality, Mothrok has many worshippers among the underground-dwelling races, and others that work with the land. Even goodly farmers spare prayers to her out of fear for their crops. As part of her control over the land, she has been known to bring forth the corpses buried within the ground and use them as undead abominations.

Nandorrin – God of Fire. Worshipped mostly by dwarven smiths, this god is also often seen as a smith. Whenever tales are heard of volcanoes running with lava, it is believed to be Nandorrin reforming part of the world. Many candle makers use his image or symbol on their work. Many wizards praise him for their destructive fire-based arcana. His clerics perform a lot of ceremonies around fire, and to an extent they can shape fire as well.

Noyugon – God of Knowledge and Learning. Often known as the "Lorekeeper", this god strives to preserve histories and knowledge, and is said to be a recorder of deeds for the gods themselves. He promotes academies and centers of learning. Needless to say, he does not have many followers outside of educated cultures.

Scriptum Verash – A Book on the Philosophies of Evil. Made by several dark gods, and by Foyul for the sake of balance, this tome is the exact opposite of *The Codex*. It details greed and lust, power and glory, and encourages the strong and cunning to take what they will. It is in every way a document of "evil", yet at the same time it also has a life of its own. These clerics practice in secret, with no room for honor or compassion. In the past they have lead armies filled with hate against enemies for no more reason than the cleric's own selfish needs.

Taekbol – God of Underworld. This dwarvish and gnomish god favors those who dwell under the ground, away from the light of the sun. This god also spreads gems and metals under the surface of the world, sometimes in competition with Mothrok's stone empire. Some human miners even claim worship to him.

Westrealei – Elven Goddess of Wind and Air. This goddess communicates with her followers by means of various flying creatures.

Her own image is painted in the shape of a pegasus, whose head and neck is replaced by the upper half of a beautiful elven female. This elven deity is of the sky, and a force of nature. Elven arrows need to ride her winds to strike true to their targets. In this respect, a windy day is said to be a bad omen for going into battle, as the archers will have a harder time hitting their targets.

Yestreal – God of the Sun and Weather. This nature deity, worshipped by many who till the soil, exerts his influence on harvests and crops. Many times this puts him in direct competition with Mothrok for the success of farmers, but the two gods were once allied during the Godswars. The sunflower is often used as his symbol. His followers often come from agricultural regions, and are generally good at farming. Clerics of this god never condone weddings on rainy days, as they feel their god shuns the marriage. Elves also have numerous followers to this nature god.

Yurtash – God of Spirits. It is hard to define what spirits are to the common man, due to superstitions and drunken fireside chats. In short, spirits are creatures neither living nor dead that perform specific tasks in the world. They are the after images of once-living creatures. While the soul may depart to another world, a part of the spirit may remain in the world, trapped, only to be harnessed by magical means. Yurtash seems to store and nurture these lost energies of forgotten souls until they have a use in the world again. Mystics, greenmen and some arcane casters call upon the spirits in spells. Many of this god's clerics share the powers of mystics over these spirits.

About the Author...

Douglas was born on Nov 28th, 1971. He got the chance to live in many different places while growing up, courtesy of the assignments the US Army offered to his father. Quiet and shy, he dreamed of other worlds and places…and desired to write about them. He got into fantasy role-playing games in his mid-teens. To this day he has friends whom he meets in tabletop role-playing games, as well as online adventures. Many of his characters evolved in games, and each developed their own personality.

Having to rely on self-publishing for his novels, Douglas was surprised at the amount of good reviews and publicity they received. The *Earthrin Stones* trilogy sold more copies than expected. *The Widow Brigade* started its reception earning ten straight 5-star reviews, including a recent widow who said it helped with her healing process.

Though Douglas expanded his entertaining to include game streams and recordings on YouTube and Twitch, his passion remains centered on his writing.

Douglas lives with his wife and two sons in Minnesota. He works in health care, serving people's needs in medical imaging. When most people see him, he is wearing scrubs.

Learn more about the author and the Realm of Dhea Loral at…

Website – DheaLoral.com
Facebook – Dhea Loral
Twitter - @ThaminDheaLoral
YouTube - Thamin DheaLoral
Twitch: - Thamin_T

About the Cover Artist

When Douglas searched for a cover artist for The Widow Brigade, he came across the website of Obsidian Abnormal. O Abnormal has a few YouTube tutorials on artwork. He currently runs a comic on his website with regular updates. He has a commission lineup for folks wanting artwork of characters or, in this case, cover art for a book.

Fans can support him through his Patreon page, and receive special artwork and larger copies of his comic and wallpapers. His blog shares artwork, rants, The Bonebreakers, tutorials and more.

For more information, check out his artwork-based Twitch broadcasts at https://www.twitch.tv/oabnormal

About the Editor

Denise Guibord is a freelance editor and writer who loves the creative process in nearly all crafts from writing to knitting to painting. As an editor, she works with authors to tighten up scenes and descriptions, smooth out punctuation and mechanics, and guide the project to bridge its layers of connecting details, all while honoring the author's original voice and intention. Her website is www.deniseguibord.com

Want to experience more of the world of Dhea Loral? Explore the dwarf homelands through the eyes of revolutionary Duli! *The Widow Brigade* opened on Amazon with seven critiques praising the story, and each giving it a perfect 5 stars! This story features strong women, in a fantasy setting, rebelling against the traditions of a male-dominated society.

"I felt the plot was well developed, well paced, and the motivations of the characters really drew me in, caring about what happened as the plot progressed. I felt the main character was not your typical shiny hero, or dastardly anti-hero. She just felt real. I highly recommend this book..." - Tom H

"This book is very well written and as always with his stories, the battle scenes are intense, with details that pull you in and fully immerse yourself in the story. The characters are well developed and allow you to enjoy loving and hating them." – Lockhart

Discover the series which introduced fantasy readers to the realm of Dhea Loral. The *Earthrin Stones* trilogy gives the reader the largest backstory and plot driving the scenes of this world. Open your adventure with *Inheritance of a Sword and a Path*!

"Over a thousand years ago the Godswars ravaged the land of Dhea Loral, shattering continents, laying waste to cities, and driving species to extinction. The people of the land are once again starting to prosper and flourish, while the gods stay aloft and watch from afar the recovery. Yet, not all the old quarrels have been forgotten. For some gods, the time is right to once again meddle in the affairs of mortals. Though the gods have bound themselves by a Covenant that bars their direct entry into Dhea Loral, they are able to send mortal emissaries to carry out their schemes."

"*Inheritance of a Sword and a Path* is a treasure trove of fantasy, eye-popping adventures, lead characters imbued with morality, humility, strength and humor…This saga opener had me turning pages, reading way (way) past my bedtime, and definitely curious for the next installment. Pure fun!" — Lori Crever "30 Minutes with the Author"

Next in the Pilgrims with Blades series:

A02 Grandfather's Castle

9 781949 060010